The Human Act
and
Other Stories

Angela Lam

ISBN: 9780988542754

Library of Congress Control Number: 2012955978

Cover design by All Things That Matter Press

Published in 2013 by All Things That Matter Press

Foreword

I am grateful to the editors who have worked with me over the years, especially Pam McCully and Kathryn Morrison at *Lynx Eye* magazine for publishing my first short story, "Queen of Jingle Junk," and inviting me to represent the magazine at the San Francisco Book Festival. Special thanks to Jinx Beers at *Lesbian Short Fiction* who taught me how to write characters readers care about. Beers originally purchased both "Fistful of Love" and "Friends" but returned the rights to both stories once the publication folded and sent a very generous kill fee along with a handwritten note wishing me much success with my future literary endeavors.

I thank my family for their loving patience and continual support of my writing throughout the years. We have encountered many adventures on the journey, from traveling to Del Mar for a job interview at a literary agency to childcare arrangements allowing me to attend residencies at Hedgebrook and the Vermont Studio Center. Special thanks to my husband, Ed, who has spoken on my behalf at readings and book signings and who has endured the many questions from curious readers throughout the years.

To the readers many thanks for supporting my work. Without you, there would be no reason to share these stories.

Table of Contents

Ashes to Angels

On the Friday before I quit smoking, I met up with Libby and Davies at the 7-Eleven immediately after school. It was hot, almost summer, and Davies had a pack of Marlboros rolled into a sleeve of her white T-shirt. Libby slumped beside the glass doors, fidgeting with the buttons on her pink blouse, staring at her worn Keds. When I approached, Davies handed Libby two cigarettes and asked her which she wanted to do first: movies or the mall.

"Count me in," I said.

"You bring your money?" Davies asked, arching a dark eyebrow.

"I'll pay you next week. I'm short on cash."

"That's what you said last week." Davies crossed her tan arms over her broad chest. She was a wrestler. She wasn't one to let up on anyone for anything.

I nudged Libby under the ribs, hoping she'd loan me the money.

"Sorry," Libby said, taking a drag from her cigarette. "I only got enough for me."

"You can't pay, you can't stay," Davies said.

I grabbed Libby's cigarette. "Consolation prize," I hissed. I blew a puff of smoke into Davies' face. "Next time cheat from yourself."

After stalking three blocks, a sleek candy-red Nova stopped in front of me. Someone rolled down a window and shouted, "Adele." The driver was Rhoda Stewart, a dull, unattractive girl whose parents pampered her like she was a princess.

Rhoda squinted in the sunlight. "I've been meaning to talk to you. I heard you got an A on the last trig test."

"Yeah, so."

"I was wondering if you could help me. My mom's on my case. I'll pay you."

"Fifty an hour," I said, hoping the steep price would deter her. I wanted to be alone.

"Get in." The passenger's door popped open.

I slipped into the cool interior and felt the white leather mold against my back and legs, an odd sort of comfort. Rhoda eyed me.

"The cigarette has to go," she said. "My mom's allergic to smoke and this is her car. She'll kill me."

"You're kidding."

"Her name's on the pink slip till after I graduate from college."

Rhoda revved the engine, her eyes on the trail of smoke wafting from between my fingertips.

I thought about the cash, fifty an hour. It would get me out of debt with Davies and put a pack of cigarettes in my pocket for weeks. I rolled down the window. The red-tipped glow bounced down the street.

***

Rhoda Stewart lived in Montecito Heights in a rambling two-story home with white shutters and a wraparound porch. When I stepped out of the Nova, I sneezed from the fragrance of pine needles and licorice plants. Black crows chattered and swooped from the treetops and lemon-yellow sunlight flickered through the branches. I felt like I had walked into one of those quaint country pictures hanging in the classier restaurants downtown, from a long time ago, of some place you only read about, that doesn't exist anymore.

Our footsteps echoed in the wide marble entry. Sun-drenched walls and cathedral ceilings reminded me of church where there were rules: no drinking, no smoking, no cheating, no lying. Things that had never been asked of me.

Rhoda's room was as spacious and quiet as the rest of the house. An oak dressing table with a make-up set and hot rollers leaned against the wall. Shuttered doors opened into a walk-in closet with racks of jeans and dress shirts and a row of shoes lined neatly under them. A poster of Jason Priestly hung on the ceiling above the bed crowded with stuffed animals, and when I closed the door, a life-sized poster of Cindy Crawford, wet in a yellow swimsuit, stared back at me.

"I want to be a supermodel," Rhoda explained. "But my mom wants me to be a lawyer like her."

Rhoda tossed her backpack on the floor and slumped into a giant white beanbag. I didn't carry any books. On Fridays I always left them in my locker to collect dust, hoping to catch some fun to make up for the rest of the week.

I sat on the floor and crossed my legs. It was so quiet I could hear my thoughts bounce around in my head. "So, what are you having problems with?" I asked.

"Slopes. I can't figure out which axis is which. I mean, in theory I do, but my mind goes blank under pressure."

"That's easy. X lays down. Y stands up."

"How do you remember it, though?"

I couldn't tell her how I remembered things by the power of

association. I woke some nights to my mother's voice in the kitchen. "I spend half my life laying down with strangers." So, I changed it. "You said your mother's a lawyer, right? X is a woman *laying down* the law. Y is a man who has to *uphold* it. Okay?"

Rhoda nodded.

She handed me her book and we went over things: probability, parabolas, polynomials. An hour passed. Two. Someone rapped on the door. A head poked in. "Who's your friend?" the woman asked.

"Adele. This is my mom." Rhoda motioned to the woman who shared the same dark hair and eyes, though she was thinner, prettier, with a genuine warmth and a firm handshake.

"Pleased to meet you. Would you care to stay for dinner? I'll have Maria set an extra plate if you do. It's no trouble."

Our eyes met and I thought of my mother at my age, dropping out of high school to marry my father, giving birth to me three days before her sixteenth birthday. She settled into a trailer on the avenue. Down here, dust from the interstate kicked through the chain-link fence and stung your eyes. The only money came from working the streets, the clubs or the Social Security office on Cleveland. The only reprieve from the heat was a six-pack of beer and a block of ice.

"No, thank you. Maybe some other time." I lied. It was a habit by now, less demanding than honesty. "My mother works down the street. She's off at six. I'll meet her at the office." Another lie. My heart shrank.

"Let me drive you," Mrs. Stewart said. "The road's steep."

"No, thank you," I said, my voice edged with persistence. "I'd rather walk."

Rhoda and her mother escorted me to the gravel driveway. Mrs. Stewart chatted briefly about herself, about working as a family law attorney for children of divorce and abuse, about the sad cases she heard every day, and how she strove to help even the worst ones. Then she asked me questions about my life, questions I refused to answer. The silence between us widened, and Rhoda stepped in to fill the space. "She's really good in math, Mom. She's helping me in trig." Rhoda gasped. "That reminds me. I owe you a hundred dollars."

"Here, Rhoda, let me split the difference with you." Mrs. Stewart withdrew two twenties and a ten from her leather purse. Rhoda ran into the house and came back with another fifty.

I wadded the bills and shoved them into the front pocket of my shorts. When we were near the street, Mrs. Stewart took my hand, held it a long moment, "Thank you again for helping Rhoda. She needs someone intelligent like you as a role model in math. It's the one subject where she lacks confidence."

I glanced away, afraid of my heart expanding, opening with possibilities.

"Remember to ask your mother if you can stay for dinner on Monday," Mrs. Stewart said. "We're having veal."

I nodded, the first truth born in silence.

***

On the way home I stopped at a twenty-four-hour deli and almost slipped a pack of cigarettes into my pocket before remembering I had money. At the mall, I pocketed a set of faux ruby earrings, then thought better of it, and paid for them at the counter. The cashier gave me a gift box. The gold wrapping paper gleamed in my hands.

At nine-thirty, as I waited for my mother to return, I walked into my bedroom, pressed a milk crate under my window, climbed up and spread my arms into a Y. A slight breeze created a whirlpool of moving heat, the illusion of relief. I crawled down from the milk crate and hunched against the mattress, listening to the familiar sounds of gunshots and sirens. There was no place to go. I would wait for my mother.

At 3:30 a.m. my mother's keys fumbled in the lock. Her heels clattered against the linoleum. She stumbled into the kitchen and tossed her purse on the card table.

I walked out of my bedroom to join her in the kitchen.

"I'm tired," she said, her voice weak with self-pity.

It had been a bad night, I was sure, and whatever had happened was not something she wanted to confide in anyone, especially a daughter whom she sometimes hated, sometimes envied.

I pulled up a chair and sat down beside her. The vinyl upholstery creaked like the bones of an old woman and stuck like gum to the backs of my thighs. From my pocket I withdrew the tiny gold box and slid it across the table.

"For me?"

I nodded.

Her long chipped nails ripped into the gold paper. She stared at the ruby earrings. A frown cut craters into the full moon of her face. "What boy gave these to you?"

"I bought them."

"With what money?"

I took seventy crumpled dollars from my pocket and smoothed them on the table.

My mother's lips tightened in anger. "Slut." She smacked my cheek with a blunt palm. Her fingers snaked against my skin.

"I earned it."

"I know how you earned it and I don't like it. Not one bit. Just 'cause I do it don't make it right."

"It's not like that."

"Yeah, yeah, yeah, that's what they all say, at first."

Tears welled up in my eyes and I tried to think of how to put what I was feeling into words. "I used my brains, not my body."

"Gambling? Takes no more brains to lose money than it does to earn it. Let me tell you that."

"Studying, Mama. I was studying."

"Studying what?"

"Trigonometry." She frowned. "Math." Her face lightened.

I fought back tears and struggled to make the words come out of my mouth. "Rich girl from school paid me to teach her. Paid me. And her mother wants me to come back for dinner next week. I told her I would ask you. May I?" I wanted my mother to know that what I was doing was different from what she thought.

"Sure, honey," my mother said sarcastically. "Ain't nothing better than taking money from rich folks, I hear. Less money for them to sin with."

"Mrs. Stewart's a lawyer. She fights for justice."

"Don't go talking to me about justice and lawyers. They ain't helped make your daddy pay for a roof over your head."

I stood up. Out of the ashes, an angel had risen and given me hope and I was not about to let my mother take it away from me. "Mrs. Stewart's not like that."

My mother pulled herself up from the chair, a withering woman with not much left of either beauty or grace. "That's what they all say."

Her voice smarted. She disappeared down the hall. I heard the bedroom door open and close; the springs of the mattress squeak as she adjusted herself on the bed.

My throat itched. I fumbled in my mother's purse for a match. Then I remembered something important, something Rhoda had told me. "My mom's allergic to smoke." I sat down and stared at the earrings. The small stones smoldered like the red-tipped glow of cigarettes. I snapped the box shut and slipped it into my pocket along with the cash. I didn't care what my mother said, I was going to Rhoda's house on Monday for dinner.

Fistful of Love

With my purple gym bag in one hand, wet bikini and towel in the other, I hustled past the white apartments with their Spanish tile roofs. It was a Friday evening in late July in the middle of the worst heat wave north of Los Angeles. I had just finished a deliciously long swim at Hyde Community Pool. My thongs flapped against pavement. I was hoping to beat Kate home. We'd had another one of our fights before Kate had left for work and I was banking on avoiding another confrontation by greeting her with freshly tossed Caesar salad and cold beer when she stepped in through the front door.

The argument was the same old thing: Kate was restless and I was tired of moving. In the flush of new love, after two drinks and one night of knowing each other, we decided to move in together. I had been living alone for five years since graduating from college, and the loneliness of a cramped studio apartment in the fringes of a hustling city ached deep in my bones. But the one dream we had together—of finding a place to call home—had never materialized in the five moves we had made in the nine months we had been together. Each time Kate promised, "This is it. We're staying," and then weeks later, if not evicted for breaking ground rules such as no loud music after ten, Kate would suggest, "Let's move," over something insignificant, a missing morning paper or a diaper discarded two feet from a trash can. Sometimes after another one of our spats I began to think maybe her old lover was justified in leaving. The thought fleeted under the oppression of loneliness, its memory as fresh as rain in a desert, and I decided to stay.

We had been living in the same downstairs apartment for one month. Just last week the landlord had selected the all American couple out of the pages of a 1950's copy of *Ladies' Home Journal* to live directly above us. When a man bent his burly back over a lumpy mattress to unload two sides of a crib, Kate groaned, "Ugh! A family!" I was biding my time, wondering how many days I had before I needed to pack my clothes and call a moving van.

I turned into the shadeless blue and white complex where a nest of children swarmed on Rollerblades. It was about seven-thirty but it was hot—the type of heat where your thighs stick together and rub the skin raw. The rooms of the apartments, incubators of separate, private hells, were empty. Women sat on street curbs watching their children cycle figure eight's in the street. Men pulled their clunkers into the carport and unloaded six packs. They kissed their women who fumbled in their back pockets searching for paychecks. Occasionally, someone would dart into an open door and slide into a kitchen to grab some lemonade. Refrigerators opened and shut, hungry mouths breathing in coolness, the only relief from the sweltering southern California paradise.

We lived too far from the beach, too close to the desert, and the rush of evening traffic from the main artery onto the freeway was punctuated by the screams and laughter of children. Burnt chicken and ribs and charcoal saturated the thick gauzy air. And, even after a shower, I still smelled of chlorine and suntan lotion.

Kate's red truck was not parked under the carport. I sighed with relief. I had time, how much I didn't know, but I decided to stop at the mail slots. Maybe Carnival Comics had written to tell me they liked my strips and wanted to see more. Maybe, cross my fingers, they wanted me on their staff of artists.

"Excuse me," said a woman, "but the landlord said there's a washer and dryer in the complex." A pair of green eyes peered up at me from beneath a white wicker basket of T-shirts and underwear. The woman was small, I guessed no taller than four feet and seven inches, with a cloud of blond hair and hands as tiny as dove's wings. She looked swollen with grief. Her distended abdomen tugged at the seams of a shapeless denim maternity frock. Her arms were covered with a light yellow down. I thought she couldn't be older than twenty-five, but her face was heavily made-up, especially around the eyes which were slightly puffy as if from lack of sleep.

I mustered a grin. "Over there, behind the blue door." I pointed to the rectangular plywood door with its vented slats like the gills of a fish. The humidity was so dense it coalesced on the door. Its worn and weary paint-job harassed by cobwebs.

The woman crinkled her nose, her hands balancing the armload of clothes, and she sneezed. Her head bobbed. A man's well-worn Fruit of the Loom underwear fell on the cement path of the breezeway. I stooped to retrieve it, the elastic soft and stretched beyond its original shape, and tossed it back into the basket perched on the woman's head.

"Thanks—"

"Sara." I held out my hand, the palm sweaty and warm. "Apartment one." I nodded to the door beside the laundry room.

The blond woman dropped her gaze. I thought she might be distrustful of my outstretched hand, but she shifted the weight above her head so she could give me her hand.

"I'm Jean." Our hands clasped in a friendly new neighbor embrace. I knew how strange and awkward it felt moving to a new place and I wanted Jean to feel welcomed. A dank, musty smell lifted from her talcum powder skin. The rich aqua green of her eyes shifted like waves, ebbing and flowing around the dark pupils and pooling around the rims, tumultuous sea green eyes. "Is it always this hot?" she asked.

I shook my head; my voice lodged in my throat. Something about her arrested me. Kate's fresh-scrubbed look and arrogant composure starkly contrasted to Jean's carefully made-up pale features. I thought of a cartoon character I had created, the one Kate disdainfully referred to as Pooh-Pooh Princess, a hapless woman with Rapunzel-like hair and teardrop eyes who waved a handkerchief from a castle turret waiting to be rescued by a knight in shining armor. I imagined Jean as my character and began inventing a narrative to ease my anxiety over Kate's pending arrival.

"It's a roaster upstairs." Jean's shrill voice grated like nails against a chalkboard. "I've been rubbing ice cubes over my wrists to keep cool."

Behind us, the sun's down pouring on the horizon smeared gold and cotton candy pink streaks through a misty lavender sky. It was getting closer to eight o' clock and cooler weather. At least the glare would be off the pavement and the children would go indoors to wrestle in front of their color TVs or tumble into bed. They'd kick off the covers and lay spread-eagle on top of cotton sheets trying desperately to get some sleep. Their bodies would toss and turn, being wound up from too much sun and too much sugar.

"It'll be cooling soon," I said. "Where are you from?"

"Washington. Lots of green. Lots of water." Jean glanced furtively around. Her harsh voice lowered a notch. "But no jobs."

I nodded. I didn't want to tell her I was an unemployed cartoonist since Fantasy Comics folded last month. "Welcome to California," I said. "Let me know if you need anything, we like to help."

Jean squinted in the sunlight. "I don't know which is worst, the heat or driving three days straight. Anyway, it's good to be home."

Home. Spoken by Jean, the word intensified my longing. I started daydreaming of a faraway place in the cool clouds where every day was like the last, completely comfortable in the familiarity knitted over being in the same place for a long, long time. No more boxes. No more moving vans. No more first, last, and security deposit. No more strangers entering and leaving through the revolving door of our lives.

A cinnamon red Chevy lumbered into the carport. Kate leaned into her horn, the stereo blaring AC/DC's "Highway to Hell." A seven-year-old boy threw a rubber ball against the Chevy's steel bumper. Kate rolled down the window and shouted, "Hey! Stay away from my truck!" Kids scattered like marbles, hiding in the shrubs beside the building or under the protective umbrella of their mothers' arms.

Kate jumped out of the cab and slammed the door. Jean's gaze darted from Kate to the blue laundry room door. Her skittish green eyes reminded me of a cat caught in headlights, alternatively dazzled and paralyzed by fear and fascination. I sidestepped from the mail slots to allow room for her to pass. Jean's right hand steadied the basket of clothes perched on her head. She bit her lower lip and fumbled with the doorknob. I should have helped her, but I didn't think about it until it was too late. Her silent independence seduced me, and I found myself embarrassingly shy around her. Jean apparently didn't notice this. She set the bundle of clothes on top of the dryer and closed the door.

"God, am I glad to be home," Kate said, kissing my cheek. She had apparently forgotten our earlier argument; at least, her sweetness was deceiving. "Randy promised us overtime, and boy, did he deliver! No problem with rent this month."

Kate smiled, but I didn't notice.

Jean emerged from the laundry room and tottered up the stairs, one step at a time, her slender back hiding the protruding package in front of her. I imagined folding my arms around her waist and being pleasantly surprised by the tight fullness of her tummy.

"Who's that?" Kate asked.

"Our new neighbor."

The heat shimmered where Jean had stood. I found myself wondering what her skin might taste like in this ninety-degree humidity. Would it be salty and bite like a margarita, or would it be pasty and bitter like dry, stale basil? She was no stranger to the flesh, her burgeoning belly attested to her experience, yet I wondered if she had ever kissed a woman with those deliciously pink lips, and part of me trembled to think she might have.

I stood in the breeze way and absently shuffled through the mail: three bills, a body building magazine for Kate, and an offer for yet another weekend course on painting for me. There was no letter from Carnival Comics. My gaze followed Jean up the stairwell.

"She seems nice," I told Kate.

Kate winked and unlocked our front door. "Let's see if she likes Zeppelin."

***

I hadn't considered letting anyone know of my feelings for Jean, especially since she was married to Jack, a hulking man with broad hands and stubby fingers callused from repairing stalled cars and installing new engines. His massive forehead and wide-set eyes led me to believe he thought little and felt much, though he had no words in which to express himself. His slight grunts, whenever he had the mind to return my greeting on the few occasions we met at the mail slots, only confirmed this belief.

On Thursday evening I sat with my legs curled under my hips on the beige sofa while flipping through the classifieds. Kate hummed from the kitchen. The portable fan oscillated from where it was strategically placed in the hall blowing hot air from one end of the apartment to the other. Jean's distinctive plunk, plunk footsteps echoed from the stairwell. My heart thundered to the beat of each step. I folded the newspaper in half and tiptoed to the front door. Through the peephole, Jean's golden head bowed beneath a mountain of underwear and T-shirts. I never saw her any other time, and for a while, I wondered if all she ever did was wash clothes.

"What are you doing, Sara?" Kate asked.

I spun around, wide-eyed, back slouched against the closed door, hands helplessly stuffed into pockets. I fumbled for an excuse. "I … I thought … I heard something. And I thought it was Mr. Keith."

"What would he be doing here?" Kate demanded. "I paid your half of the rent."

"I know," I stammered. "But, sometimes I worry."

"There's no need to worry. I've kept the stereo low. I didn't smack the kid who turned over the garbage cans." Kate's eyebrow arched inquisitively. "I promised, remember?"

"Yes, I remember."

"So, don't worry about it," Kate said. I wondered if her good mood would last the entire evening. Kate had finished a roofing job early and had been paid a hefty bonus. No matter how much we argued for security's sake, Kate didn't trust banks. She stuffed the wad of twenties in the bottom of a tea tin kept on the top shelf of a cupboard. We'd need the extra cash if I didn't find work by winter.

Although Kate hadn't mentioned my unemployment, it rubbed between us like a splinter under skin. I moved away from the door to the far right corner of the room where my drafting table and office chair sat unoccupied for weeks. I picked up the last sketch I had worked on. The steel tip of a sword pierced what should have been a dragon's heart, but its blade waved aimlessly through air. I hadn't been inspired to finish it.

"Good drawing," Kate said, leaning over my shoulder. "Have you heard from Carnival Comics?"

"They're not hiring."

"Don't worry. Just keep sending out your strips. Somebody's bound to buy one." She patted my shoulder, then nodded toward the dragon. "Are you going to finish it?"

"I haven't been inspired."

"You of all people know you can't wait around for inspiration. You need to create it." Kate winked and sauntered back into the kitchen where she diced mushrooms, tomatoes, and green onions and tossed them in a bed of romaine lettuce.

The laundry door creaked. I turned to glance out the peephole. Jean's golden hair seemed to glow disproportionately large, a beacon flashing once across the darkness. I strolled over to the drafting table and flipped through my artist's journal. I thought of the knight and the dragon. Pandering to the public, I never considered drawing anything for myself, not since college when I decided to become a commercial artist. Long sleepless nights I sketched other people's dreams: heroic men and helpless women or warrior women without a touch of softness to them. Then Jean's blond head, with one swooping streak, illuminated the bareness of my creative life. I'd construct a tower for my dauntless heroine, Princess Jean. I grabbed a pencil and flipped to a blank page.

"Whatcha drawing?" Kate set a bowl of salad on top of the TV and turned on the stereo.

"Nothing." I placed Jean's profile face down on the drafting table, picked up the bowl, and seated myself on a folding metal chair at the card table in the dining area. Kate stared at me intently. Between the walls, water flowed through pipes. I imagined Jean washing dishes. In my fantasy, I stood below the open window and cupped my hands around the O of my mouth and called out, "Jean, oh, Jean, let down your long hair." Jean pulled back the dingy drapes and threw down the long golden rope of hair. I climbed in and held her in my arms, including her baby belly, and pressed tender kisses onto her pink lips.

"It's good to see you're drawing," Kate said. There was an air of practicality in her voice, which I interpreted as renewed hope for my future employment.

I blushed, not thinking of my career as an artist, but of the deliciously rich feelings Jean aroused in me. And, though Kate didn't mention it, I know she noticed my gaze turned inadvertently toward the front door when a half hour later Jean's wobbly steps plodded down the stairs.

***

Things seemed to be going well with our new neighbors. We hadn't had a phone call from Mr. Keith in a while and I had begun to entertain the thought of putting up real curtains in place of the yellow blinds. On a brave day, I decorated the egg white walls with copies of the fantasy posters I had drawn over the years, mostly wizards and fairies in cool, dreamy pastels, with delicate, transparent, silver-tipped wings shrouded in star-kissed clouds.

I sat at my drafting table on a Saturday morning contemplating the next addition to Jean's castle, an intricate labyrinth of spires and turrets and courtyards. Outside, an ice cream truck played *Pop Goes the Weasel.* Children darted between parked cars, spraying water on each other from plastic squirt guns. Behind the fence, Kate yelled something to someone. There was a clash of metal against concrete. I reflexively slid the charcoal castle under a stack of pen and ink drawings when I heard Kate slam the front door.

Kate's gaze slipped from my drafting table to meet my startled eyes. "That guy, Jack, had the audacity to roll our bin to the curb when he saw me carrying the garbage out." Kate loomed beside me. Her brown face flushed red with exaggerated exasperation. "And not only did he do that, but he stopped to grab the bag I was carrying. The nerve!"

"Did you let him?" I asked. To Kate's strong disapproval, I still enjoyed the opening of doors and "Ladies first" attitude some men demonstrated.

"Of course not! We wrestled over that bag and I won!" Kate smirked, the crooked smile betraying mischievous glee. "The bag ripped and everything fell out, but what the hell, I won. And, no, I didn't let him pick it up either."

I wiped my blackened hands in a rag and sharpened a pencil. Through the open sliding glass door, heat slithered in, dense and oppressive. The walls heaved exhausted sighs. I was getting tired of Kate's adolescent defiance which I had, at first, found endearing, especially when she slammed a guy's face into a bar counter when he told me to screw him for not accepting the drink he had bought me. Months later, it was no longer amusing. "He was only trying to be kind.

Isn't it okay for guys to be kind once in a while?"

"There's a difference between being kind and being chauvinistic."

"You're not in Idaho anymore. Guys aren't automatically chauvinistic when they're being nice."

Kate clenched her fists. A look of hurt surprise flitted across her face. She had grown up in Idaho and had left impulsively one night, driving across two states to escape the pain of being left by a woman. "I'm sorry, Kate. I didn't mean to say that." I tapped the end of my pencil against the drafting table, calming exacerbation. "I'm sure he was just being nice."

The creases softened in Kate's face. Her shoulders slackened and her fists uncurled. "I'm sorry, Sara. It's just this damn heat. It makes me irritable."

"No kidding. You're worse than when I'm having PMS."

Kate ignored the comment and disappeared into the shower. The rush of pulsating water plunked through the pipes in the wall. It was a familiar, though annoying sound. With trembling fingers, I withdrew the picture of Jean's castle. I hadn't seen Jean in weeks, not since I stopped gazing out the peephole, but occasionally I heard her humming upstairs in the kitchen or padding across the living room floor. I picked up a piece of charcoal and smeared black into varying shades of gray, creating a light tulle fog. Upstairs, a shrill scream pierced the fabric of silence, followed by a quick succession of thumps, and muffled sobbing. "My God, he's hitting her!" I thought. The stubby piece of charcoal fell from my parted fingers. My heartbeat knocked against my ribs. I wanted to pick up the phone and call the police, but I couldn't move. My eyes stared blankly at the half-finished sky.

"What are you drawing?" Kate asked, a towel wrapped around her body and tucked under her arms.

"Did you hear that?" I asked.

"Hear what?"

"I thought I heard them fighting."

Kate shrugged and vigorously rubbed her short, no-nonsense crop of brown hair with a hand towel. "So, couples fight all the time. Even we fight."

"But not like what I thought I heard. He was, I meant it sounded like, he was beating her." The words fell heavy and flat from my astonished lips.

Kate scrunched up her lips in disgust. "What did I tell you? That son of a—"

"I could be wrong," I stammered, feeling the heat of Kate's anger bristling under her freshly scrubbed skin. I didn't want Kate storming up the stairs and pounding on the neighbor's front door and having them phone Mr. Keith about the impropriety of our nosiness. And then, having Kate fly off into another rage, phoning Mr. Keith and accusing him of not caring about the welfare of his tenants. Most of all, I didn't want to have to look for another place to rent. I wanted some peace.

Kate threw the hand towel on the shaggy carpet and slipped into a pair of jeans and pulled an inside out T-shirt on backwards over her head. Forget the shoes, Kate stomped toward the door.

I pressed my back against the wood and stretched my arms across the doorjamb.

"What are you doing?" Kate asked. It was the first time I had dared to intercede.

"I said I could be wrong."

Upstairs, a volley of punches pummeled into soft skin. Kate glared at me with furious brown eyes. "Get out of my way." Her hands braced me under the armpits. I knew she could lift all one hundred and five pounds of me with the ease of someone who's accustomed to bench-pressing one hundred and fifty pounds at the gym. I wasn't afraid. Kate never hurt me, her intention was always to get me out of the way, but I didn't want her to interfere this time.

"I don't care if she's married to him," Kate said. "She doesn't need to put up with that abuse!"

"But you can't save her." Truth was I wanted to save Jean. If I hadn't been terrified by the hulking brute and had possessed Kate's eternal sense of self-confidence, I probably would have. But I didn't.

Kate's fingers tightened under my arms. "Move or I'll move you."

Upstairs, the crying had stopped immediately after the door banged. Feet thundered down the stairs. The engine of the gray pick-up coughed, then roared. Its clanking awkwardness sputtered out of the carport. Then silence.

Kate pursed her lips, the creases in her forehead disappeared. She slipped her hands out from under my armpits and turned toward the bathroom to comb her hair. "Next time," Kate said.

I sighed, dazed and relieved, hoping there wouldn't be a next time.

That night I lay awake with my hands folded over my chest while Kate snored beside me. I listened to lumbering footsteps ascend the stairs, the click of the front door, Jean's shrill voice, Jack's meek rumble. I couldn't make out the words, but the tone shifted from subtle hostility to stifled gentleness, an ensemble of apologies and forgiveness. I rolled over and closed my eyes, but couldn't sleep. I thought of Jean lying beside me, my arms snug around her swelling abdomen, my cheek against her golden hair.

Kate snorted and woke up. She rolled over and touched my folded hands. "Sara." Kate's voice was urgent. "I had a nightmare that you left me."

I lay still in my nightgown and Kate continued. "I came home and your drawings were off the walls and there was a note—"

"It was only a dream," I reassured her.

"God, Sara, it felt real." Her voice was soft, almost tender. "I've lost many things, you know, including my mother, and I don't like the idea of losing anything more. I'm not smart, you know, I never finished college, but I'm not stupid either. I know the things people do when they're in love and I know you've been doing them, and not for me." The last phrase she added with a sense of finality that did not escape me. "I know you haven't found work, but when you do, are you planning on leaving me?"

I stiffened, knowing Kate had been left by Deedee, the only other woman she had ever loved.

"Why would I leave?"

"Because I'm not a helpless princess like that girl trapped in that castle you're drawing. For Jean."

"Kate," I said, rolling over so that my back faced her. "I don't know what you're talking about."

"I think you do know, but I also think you're scared of me becoming angry." Her hand moved to the hollow curve of my side. It rested firmly in the crook between my ribs and my hip. "I'm sorry I'm the way I am, I can't help it, growing up with a bunch of hicks who think nothing of women and having to always prove myself, even now, even in California. I know you can't understand it. You've always lived here and people are nice to you even if they don't mean it. But, it's different with me and you know it. I have to stand for something. Always. And some people don't like it."

I felt Kate wasn't entirely right. I may have lived in California all my life but never in the same place twice. My father was stationed in Monterey for three years, Silicon Valley for five years, and along the coast of southern California for ten. We never bought a house. I remembered sitting on my mother's lap flipping through Sears catalog for a dining table. We moved before she could buy it.

Kate let her hand slip from my side. She was silent for a moment. The air hung heavy between us. "I just want to know if you're thinking of leaving."

"No, I'm not."

"But you love her?"

I scooted further to the edge of the bed, and pulled the strings of my nightgown tighter, close around my neck. "I don't have the luxury of choice, Kate. She's married. She's having a baby." That wasn't all of it, not the whole reason, but it was all I wanted to say.

"Deedee was married when I met her." I was surprised and didn't reply. The heat seemed to thicken in the darkness, as if a dragon breathed in the space between us, and if I turned my head, I'd be looking down into its flaming throat. I should have known there was another reason for her anger.

"But I loved her just the same," said a voice from faraway. Kate spoke as if she was going to cry.

I felt pity, the same pity I had felt when we first met and Kate told me about Deedee. I was surprised Kate still needed me to rescue her from the memory of another woman, even more surprised that she was haunted by the possibility of losing me.

"Kate, if we have to move, we're moving together, just as always."

"Sara, I *do* love you even though I'm not as soft as you might like." I said nothing, the steady breathing of the invisible dragon strong against my back. "But, you do love her?"

I felt tightness in my chest, something hard and unyielding like stone. Fear and fascination, the same look I had seen mirrored in Jean's eyes the first time we met, bubbled up into my throat, making it difficult for me to speak. Perspiration soaked through the thin nightgown and suddenly I wished I was naked, though part of me felt I already was.

"I swear I won't be angry," Kate said, "if you tell the truth."

I rolled over—the dragon gone—and cupped Kate's brown face silhouetted in moonlight. I kissed her lips once, twice. "Let's not talk about it. It doesn't matter how I feel; I want to be with you."

The next two weeks I didn't hear anything although I saw Jack and Jean leave the apartment once or twice to buy groceries. Then the following week, the anticipated cries of a newborn reverberated down the thin walls.

***

It was early September and a northern wind promised to lop the edge off the unbearable heat. It never came. The sky deepened into a listless blue. The sun, a fiery inertia, haunted the empty streets where children, now in school, once played hide n' seek. I had sold a few black and white drawings to a small advertising agency but hadn't found any consistent work. Although Kate didn't say anything, I suspected the sharpness of her tongue reflected an uneasy suspicion of my continuing unemployment.

A week after the baby was born, Kate and I retired in front of the TV to watch *The Tonight Show*. The blinds had been drawn to keep the place cooler. The portable fan blew warm air against our faces. I nestled close to Kate, leaning my head against her shoulder. She had just showered, coming home late from a roofing job, and smelled of aloe and shampoo. Kate's fingers combed through the tangles of my hair. In the middle of a joke, the baby wailed, and both Kate and I missed the punch line. The baby's cries rollercoastered, one piercing shriek dipping into a low whimpering grovel before ascending to an even sharper, meaner pitch.

"You wish they had volume control," Kate said, pointing upstairs. Kate aimed the remote and Jay Leno's laughter reached a distorted decibel.

"Stop that!" I grabbed the remote and turned the audience's laughter into a low gush. "You don't want us to get kicked out, do you?"

Above us, Jean's sturdy legs paced the length of the hall. The baby's screams rained upon us.

Kate and I battled over the remote, alternatively raising and lowering the volume until the telephone rang. I bounced up to answer it. It was Mr. Keith. I hastily apologized for the inconsideration and promised it would not happen again, though knowing Kate, it would.

Kate smirked. "He's lucky I didn't answer the phone. You know what I would have told him."

"Yes, and we would have been evicted." I fell into the lumpy cushions and hugged a pillow. "I wish you wouldn't lose your temper like that."

"And I wish you knew when to stand up for yourself." Kate rose from the tattered beige sofa and nudged my outstretched legs with her toes. I didn't retract them. Kate snorted. "You're only doing this to annoy me. You don't have any real courage." I imagined Kate didn't know what she was talking about. Love demanded courage. It took an enormous amount of courage to love someone in all their moods, to not always say whatever came to one's mind without first thinking it through, to not snap under the whip of anger and yell or hit someone.

I immediately retracted my legs, curling them protectively under my hips. Kate chortled, "See what I mean. You'd do anything for anyone."

Kate stomped into the kitchen. The refrigerator turned itself on. Klaaaick ... mmmm. It sounded happy, secure in the knowledge that it was doing its job, keeping the food cold, even if no one noticed. Kate stalked across the nappy brown carpet and opened two bottles of Bud Light with her molars, handing one to me.

The cool beads around the neck of the moist amber bottle felt good against my warm, dry palm. Outside, crickets chirped and the low rush of traffic from the main street pulsed. The baby's cries muffled into sleep. It was almost peaceful. "I don't want to look for a new place. I like this one." I sipped my Bud and cradled my head against the pillow.

Kate slumped into the space beside me, nudging my feet away from the perimeter of her hips. She swallowed loudly and smacked her lips. "Listen, it may be quiet now, but it'll start again soon."

"Well, we just can't pick up and move whenever the mood strikes you. I'm tired of it."

"You just have a crush on what's-her-face." We hadn't mentioned Jean since the night we lay awake in bed. Kate hurtled the statement like a stone in calm water and I sat up to survey the ripples of hurt drifting from the center of unspoken longing. I didn't want to argue tonight. "I don't care what you think, Kate. I want some stability, some predictability, some permanence."

"And you think living underneath Frankenstein and Barbie and the crying kid is better than a good night's sleep?"

Kate did have a point. Sometimes it felt like we were the new parents being wakened at three in the morning for the baby's changing and feeding. And, Kate, being a light sleeper, woke up surly and didn't fall back to sleep, making it difficult for her to muster the energy to hammer nails into two by fours and lug lumber up ladders.

"You wouldn't be this way if you didn't love her." Kate stood up and slammed the empty bottle on top of the TV. The bright colors on the screen flickered.

I sat up and smoothed the wrinkles from my nightshirt, placing my half-full bottle on a cardboard coaster on the chipped coffee table. The fan oscillated, pushing dragon's breath back and forth between us. From the drafting table in the corner of the room the edges of my picture of Jean's castle fluttered whenever the fan turned its head. I had planned on framing it when I got a job. Now it seemed better if I rolled the charcoal castle up and placed it in a cardboard mailing tube and set it in the closet beside back issues of *Artist's Magazine*. I met Kate's penetrating dark gaze. "Let's not talk about it."

"Listen, you know exactly how I feel." Kate braced herself against the sixteen-inch color TV. The unearthly primary colors from the screen flamed coolly over the length of her slim body. She looked dangerous and comforting in the distance.

I rubbed my hands together, remembering what Kate had said about Deedee, how she had been married, how she had left Kate in the middle of the night, without warning and with no explanation after they had lived together for three years. And, I recalled the first night I met Kate — fresh out of Idaho, lost in California — in a bar, the red vinyl seats cracked with the stuffing coming out. Kate folded her arms on the scratched wooden counter and bent her head into the privacy of the dark cave created by her arms. Her words, muffled by sobs, recounted the details of her relationship with Deedee. I had been touched by the depth of her feeling for a woman I knew nothing about and I sensed this was someone who could also care deeply about me. Sometimes, like now, I wondered if I had been wrong. I entertained the thought of leaving, the thought of staying, balancing them back and forth like equal weights on a scale. "I said I wanted to be with you."

"But is that how you really feel? You're so secretive, hiding in your corner, drawing all the time. For all I know you two could be having an affair. God knows she doesn't work."

"She's married."

"Doesn't make a difference." Kate sauntered into the kitchen. The refrigerator door opened, jostling the glass containers of ketchup and mustard and salad dressing in the door, then slammed it shut. Kate stood in the hall, leaning her weight on her left hip, another bottle of Bud in her fist, pain creased in the lines of her forehead. "If you care so much about her, then why don't you just leave? I'm not stopping you."

"Kate, I said I wanted to be with you."

"But do you love me?"

"Of course, I do."

"Then say it. I love you."

I parted my lips. A baby wailed. Jean's shrill voice screamed something indiscernible. Feet shuffled to attend to the baby's cries.

Kate shook her head. "We're moving!" She gulped a mouthful of beer and disappeared into the hall. The colors of the room receded into black as I leaned forward and turned off the TV.

In the darkness, I closed my eyes, temporarily relieved of saying something I wasn't sure whether or not I still felt.

The next morning at breakfast I scanned the classifieds, circling prospective places to rent with a blue ballpoint pen while Kate crunched on Wheaties, her gaze transfixed by the scores listed in the sports section.

"Hey, the Dodgers are still leading! If they make it to the World Series, we're gonna have to go. I don't care how much tickets are."

"They have a room for rent for three-fifty on quiet country property ten minutes from town."

"Country property? Who said I wanted to live in the boonies?"

"I thought it might be better than having to take our chances and end up with something like this." I motioned toward the ceiling.

"But the country! What do you think I am, Betty Lou Go Milk'em Cows? Woman, you need to stop living with your head in the clouds. Get a reality check." Kate pushed back her chair; the legs grated against the vinyl floor. She tossed the dishes into the sink and scoffed. "Huh, the country. Next thing you know, I'll be coming home to Dolly Parton."

After Kate left, I opened the kitchen window. White cumulous clouds with gray underbellies drifted in the steel blue sky trapping in the swelter of the last three months. From the stereo, a male announcer stated a possibility of a northern storm front bringing cooler temperatures in the low seventies by the end of the day. I turned the spigot. Warm water rushed over the backs of my hands. I rinsed the dishes and placed them in the dishwasher.

I conjured up Jean, her short legs striding the length of the apartment every night. I couldn't explain why I loved Jean, but I knew I did. Over the last three months, I gauged my feelings for Jean by my commitment to keep the peace. Kate's sharp-witted clarity made it impossible for her to comprehend the decency of this act; she preferred, in her straightforward fashion, a confession of love.

I would not give it.

I pressed the START button on the dishwasher and retrieved the classifieds. Feet pattered above the ceiling, drowning out the lull between songs. A woman screeched, "You don't appreciate anything I do!" Several thuds. "I'm not putting up with this anymore!" Sobbing. Colicky screams. The door slammed and feet shuffled down the stairs. My heart lodged in my throat. Three knocks. I stared at the bolted door. The apartment, a passive participant, watched me with a dubious eye.

Three more knocks. They sounded urgent. I stalked across the living room without grabbing a towel to wipe my moist hands. I squinted through the peephole and glimpsed a golden halo bent into the disfiguring smallness of the lens. I opened the door, tentatively.

Purple caverns swallowed Jean's glistening sea green eyes. Her body, sturdy and compact, shivered slightly. She clutched a blue cotton sling with the infant in it. The baby soothed himself by sucking his thumb. Jean's voice, shrill and insistent, quivered with fearful desperation.

"May I use your phone?" she asked. "It's long distance."

"Yes, of course." I ushered Jean into the room, closing and locking the door more out of habit than out of fear. The room turned its skeptical eye on Jean who reeked of soiled diapers and spit-up. The princess of my fantasy had become a mother who was quickly growing ragged around the edges. It had been twelve days since we had seen each other in passing, more than twelve days since the last fight Jean had had with her husband.

Jean pressed inward, behind my robed body. Her anxious gaze seemed to stumble over the contents of the room: the furniture, sparse and mismatched, an indication of our frequent moves rather than the make-do consequence of poverty. I blushed, suddenly embarrassed by the pee-stains on the carpet, possibly from an excited puppy before the current NO PETS policy. The stereo speakers pounded out a steady rhythm of drums and electric guitars. I grabbed the remote from the coffee table, knocking over the half-full beer bottle from last night, the foam fanning like fingers across the wood surface. Forgetting Jean for a moment, I darted into the kitchen and retrieved a dish cloth to mop up the mess.

Jean stood waiting, rocking the baby in her arms, staring at the castle on the drafting table. She pivoted slowly. Her presence, saturated with heat, stank of curiosity and distrust.

"You drew that?" she asked.

"Yes, for you."

"For me?" Her voice thinned, tinged with disbelief. With the back of her hand, Jean pushed the matted hair from her forehead. The baby rubbed his face into the folds of her blue shirt.

"Well, sort of." I wrung the dishcloth in my hands, then tossed it on the coffee table. "I meant, it's what I do."

Jean's gaze returned to the princess staring out of the turret's highest window, and the mirrored reflection of the two women, one real and breathing, the other etched in charcoal. I was filled with a profound sense of fulfillment. I wanted to offer Jean a place to stay, even if it was only until Kate came home and phoned the police to have Jean file a domestic violence report, but I just stood there. Speechless.

Jean's fingers caressed the edge of the drawing. "She looks like me." Our eyes locked, an ineffable exchange of sadness, and I held my breath in hopeful recognition. The relief, brief and transitory, flitted between us, dispelling the unbearable heat of the room. Jean bowed her head, and turned away.

"Can I get you anything to drink?" I asked, suddenly the hostess.

"No, I'm fine." Jean propped the baby on her hip. Her cursory interest in the drawing drained; her gaze skittered around the room. "Where's your phone?"

I motioned her to the kitchen where the white touch-tone phone rested on the orange Formica counter beside bruised bananas and a ripe peach.

Jean lifted the receiver and punched the numbers into the keypad. There was a pause before she spat out, "Momma, Jack and I had a fight. I want to come home. No, it wasn't that kind of fight. He lost his job last week and he hit me when I was carrying the baby and, no, I haven't asked him if he's applied for unemployment. Momma, we had a fight. I don't remember what it was about. The baby's been colicky and I just want to come home. What do you mean, you won't? Yes, Momma, I know they have programs. But I want to come home. Please."

I folded my arms over my breasts and turned my back toward her, simulating the act of privacy. The refrigerator hummed. Jean hung up the receiver. Her gaze drifted from the phone book on top of the refrigerator to the window, then back to the phone. She picked up the receiver. Her fingers punched the keys. The once brightly painted fuchsia nails were dull and chipped at the ends. Jean waited, rocking the baby back and forth from hip to hip. At the last moment, she hung up.

Jean spun around on the flat soles of her shoes and casually thanked me as if I had given her a cup of sugar so she could finish baking a cake. The swift movement of her body startled me. I thought of the hulking brute and his fistful of love slamming into the side of her right cheek beneath the long lashes of her green eyes. I searched for my voice, found it. "Wait."

At first, I wasn't sure if she had heard me. My voice sounded shaky against the stretch from the kitchen where I stood to where Jean cradled the baby beside the front door.

Jean glanced back. The fan oscillated from the hall, lifting wispy strands of golden hair across the unnatural spectrum of her red and purple cheek. I strode toward her.

Jean's fingers slipped from the doorknob. She bent her head and cupped her mouth in the safety of a palm. "I've never felt so alone." Her voice cracked into a sob.

"Please stay." I reached out as though I were standing on the last rung of a ladder, fearless, though trembling, ignorant of the distance below us. I touched her shoulder.

Jean's distrustful gaze grazed the back of my hand. She bit her lower lip, the pinkness swelled, a bubble.

"No, he'll be angry," she said. Jean stepped aside and straightened her spine. Heat rushed into the vacuum. She tried to make light of it by smiling. "I'll be all right," she said, opening the door.

An unearthly chill cloaked the room, fresh as rejection. Perilously close to the blur of reality, I knew, even before Jean closed the door, that she was gone.

Outside, the sky dimmed. Shadows elongated across the carpet, much like a sleepy house cat, watching me with an insouciant eye. I shut the sliding glass door and drew the blinds. The fan hissed from the hall. I walked over to the drafting table. Tears welled up in my eyes.

I picked up the drawing. I had kept to myself most of my life, never finding a reason to make friends in school because I never knew when my father would get a call and we'd have to go. Instead, I immersed myself in a magical world of unicorns and wizards. Everywhere I went I searched for transformation: the frog who became a prince, the beast who became a man, the mermaid who became a woman. Real people didn't mean much to me unless I could change them, make them fit my fantasy. But people don't change unless they want to.

Kate was right. I needed to get my head out of the clouds. I crumpled the drawing. My fascination with rescuing Jean had absorbed the pain in my life, but it was only an alley to circumvent the embarrassment of living from cardboard boxes with a woman I no longer had anything in common with, a woman I pitied rather than loved. No matter how much I wanted Kate to trust me, she wouldn't. And no matter how much I wanted to save Jean, I couldn't. I could only save myself.

In the kitchen, I withdrew the tea tin from the top shelf of a cupboard and counted the roll of twenties. Five hundred dollars. It wasn't much, and it wasn't mine, but I felt entitled to it. I tossed a few clothes into my purple gym bag. I didn't know where I was going, but I imagined it would be quiet, without strangling heat, a place where I didn't have to prove my love to anyone, a place I could call home.

A Toast Good-Bye

After my lover threatens to kidnap my son if I ever contact him again through e-mail, love letters, phone calls, or unexpected visits, I start drinking. At first it's only in the evenings after I come home from work and have fed, bathed, and read to my two-year-old son. After I tuck him in for the night, I unscrew a strawberry wine cooler and turn on the television to relax. Eventually, after two weeks of perpetual grief, I succumb to afternoon drinks at luncheons. A girlfriend, and co-worker, asks me what's wrong. I lie and tell her I'm unhappily married. The truth is, I'm happily married, unhappily having an affair, and missing my boyfriend more than I've ever missed any other man in my life.

On the third week, the drinks start inching into the late morning hours. For a mid-morning snack, I mix a fifth of vodka with water. Sometimes I add a shot of tequila to my orange juice or a little rum to my Diet Coke.

By the end of the month I wake up thirsty for whiskey. By the time the rent is due, I'm drinking from the moment I drop the baby off at daycare to the time I pick him up at four in the afternoon. I stock up on microwave dinners and forget to buy cereal for breakfast. The kid watches television while I polish off the brandy I bought on the way home.

When the phone rings, I hug the bottle and wait. The answering machine clicks on, and the man on the other line says he's my husband. I waver momentarily. If I pick up the phone, he'll transform into my boyfriend and tell me he's coming home soon. I'll even fix him dinner. Something he loves: grilled chicken and steamed broccoli and baby carrots over a bed of wild rice. I stumble through the sea of dirty diapers and junk mail and unpaid bills and pick up the phone. "Hullo?" I mumble. The man repeats what he has already said, "It's your husband. I'll be working late. Don't wait up for me. Is everything all right?"

Of course I lie. Everything is fine, fine. I hang up before he can ask anything else. The baby has given up trying to stab the macaroni and cheese through the clear plastic coating I forgot to remove and has started crying. In a moment, I'm sobbing, too.

The light has faded, and the dark sky fills the room. The baby and I huddle in a corner, watching the flicker of the television illuminate our tears. We hold each other and rock back and forth, back and forth, mumbling like two idiots without a mother, without a father, without someone to pick us up and take us home.

Angels in Underwear

The last time I saw Randy was at his going away party. The four of us gathered at Chili's just hours before Randy's red eye flight to Bali. We requested our favorite table against the full-length plate-glass window overlooking the parking lot filled with rebuilt Mustangs and Volkswagen bugs from the Friday night crowd. In high school, we ate here once a month and knew every waitress by name. It had been seven years since our last visit, yet nothing seemed to have changed.

While my husband, Howard, used the restroom, Randy, Meg's boyfriend, ordered a drink at the bar. He didn't trust the waitress. "Screwed up one too many screwdrivers for me," he said.

Meg folded her arms against the Spanish tiles of the table. "Howard's such a nice man," Meg said wistfully. "I bet he'll make a great father."

I shrugged. I wouldn't know. "The only kids he's been around are his cousins, and they're all brats."

"But what about your sister's kids? He's great with them."

I leaned over to grab my glass of ice water and bumped my abdomen against the wooden beam of the table. I should have been used to the changing proportions of my body after seven months, but I wasn't.

A truck's high beams cut across the black pavement illuminating Meg's pale, listless body slumped over a Diet Coke. She seemed thinner, frailer, less like a heroine from a black and white movie and more like a wilting yellow rose.

"So, what are you going to do while Randy's away?" I asked.

"I don't know," Meg moaned. She twirled a strand of blond hair and twisted it behind her ear. "I always thought I'd be like you. Married. Expecting."

I blushed and glanced away. Howard strode over to the table. He was dressed in a red polo shirt, khaki slacks, and brown loafers. Change jangled in his front pockets. He bent down to peck my forehead. Meg gazed at him as if trying to solve a mystery. After all these years, Howard still had the power to captivate her. I shifted uncomfortably in the vinyl backed seat, the weight around the center of me stable and unrelenting. Howard lifted his chair and moved it closer to me so that he could sit with his right ankle draped over his left knee, his right arm hugging my shoulders. I thought he was showing off, the way cavemen used to, dragging their women by their long stringy hairs to the open fire where everyone could see. Me man, this woman, she mine, this mine, too, pointing and patting the protruding belly.

We sat under a vent. Cool air blew down against the top of my head. I rubbed my bare arms and glanced toward the bar, looking for a waitress. My glass was almost empty, and no one had taken our order.

"Hullo, hullo, hullo." Randy swaggered to the table. His John Lennon glasses reflected the lights and the people as they walked by. He balanced four glasses, two in each of his long slender hands, and set them on the blue and yellow tiles. "Rum and Cokes for everyone." He grinned and winked at me. "And a virgin for the Mum." He had bought me tomato juice.

"To Randy and Bali," Howard said, raising his glass.

I leaned back in the chair and folded my arms across my abdomen. Three glasses ticked.

"What's the matter, Mum?" Randy jostled my forearm with his elbow. "Too bloody for you?" Randy chuckled.

Howard leaned close to me. "Would you like me to order you something else?"

I shook my head. "To Randy."

"And the Mum," Randy winked.

Our glasses clicked. I sipped the tomato juice and set the glass down softly. Randy chugged the entire drink with one gulp; the knotty Adam's apple jumped in his throat.

"Anyone ready for another?" Randy slumped forward and flagged the waitress. "We're ready to order, aren't we gang?"

And though none of us had bothered to read the menu, we knew what we wanted. Meg ordered a grilled tuna salad with honey-mustard dressing on the side. Howard ordered steak and chicken fajitas and Randy ordered a bacon cheeseburger and fries. Howard usually ordered for me, something hot without meat or dairy, usually soup and a half sandwich, but since I'd been pregnant he didn't know what appealed to me anymore. "I'll have what Randy's having," I said.

Howard's left eyebrow arched and Meg stared incredulously at me. Everyone knew I was a strict vegetarian since I was fifteen and had read an article about how farmers injected drugs into cows to increase their milk productivity. In all of my food cravings, from banana and peanut butter sandwiches to ashes in a cigarette tray, I had never once hungered for meat.

Only Randy seemed pleased by the transformation. "Right on, now that woman knows how to party." Randy tipped his empty glass toward me and grinned. His lips were thin and wildly crooked as if they'd been drawn by a child who did not know how to draw a straight line.

"Hey, hey, hey. Just think. In twenty-four hours, I'll be walking on white sand, listening to the natives chant and hearing those brass kettledrums." Randy grabbed a fork and tapped the sides and rims of his empty glass. *Ting-ting-tong.* Meg slapped his wrist as if reprimanding a disruptive child. Howard covered his mouth to stifle a laugh. I smiled, amused, then frowned. There was an unaccustomed crispness in Meg's slap and I wondered what she meant by it. Meg slumped against the vinyl seat, crossed her arms over her small breasts, and stared out the window at the black sky. She seemed to smolder like a pot of water above a low flame. Randy lowered his utensils for a moment, then tapped the side of Meg's glass. *Ting!* She bolted upright. Her glare consumed the flamboyance of Randy's crooked smile.

"You're stirring up the baby," I said, cupping my hands on either side of the melon-hard protrusion. Inside, the fetus rolled, arms and legs jabbed my ribs.

"Oooooooh, let me feel." Randy didn't wait for an answer. He placed his palm on the middle of my abdomen above the navel and moved it across the surface like a doctor with a stethoscope searching for a heartbeat.

"I don't feel anything," he said.

"Right here." I moved his hand to the right, up a few inches, directly under my breast. The pressure of my fingers against Randy's slim hand remained steady and firm. My skin felt warm. My heartfelt tender. When I breathed, the back of my hand rubbed against my breast. All I had to do was remove my hand, and he'd touch me.

The baby's arm stuck out like a rolling marble under my skin.

"Whoa, how's that for a ride?" Randy withdrew his hand and tucked it under his biceps. "You're gonna have to send me a video of the little bambino coming down the chute."

"We aren't videotaping it," Howard said. He placed his hand on my knee. "Besides, I'm going to be too busying helping the doctor out, right, honey?"

"Cool." Randy bundled up his napkin into a ball and pushed his chair back. It scraped against the tile. "One, two, three, hike! Randy goes deep. Throws a pass to Howie." Randy tilted his chair back on two legs and tossed the napkin across the table and Howard caught it. "He's clear. Touch down! Home boy scores!"

Meg slapped Randy again. A red handprint bloomed on his forearm. It stung of malice and disgust. "She's having a baby, not scoring a touchdown. It's a rite of passage, a miracle of nature, one of the most profound mysteries of the universe."

"Like sex," Randy smirked.

Meg's face flushed. "No, not like sex. Is that all you think about?"

Randy burst into a deep-throated chuckle. He wrapped both arms across his chest and leaned forward. The chair legs bumped against a table leg. Randy slumped into the cavern of his folded arms. Tears squeezed out of his eyes as his body shook with rollicking laughter. Howard's restraint broke and he let out a soft roar.

"Enough already." Meg seized Randy's wrist. "Look what you're doing to Howard? Making him regress into a child. You're twenty-five for Pete's sake. Grow up."

"That's all right, Meg," I said, trying to smooth out the tension.

"No, it's not all right, Judy. You're my friend, and this is … *was* … my boyfriend. If he can't respect an expectant mother, then I don't know who he can respect."

"What do you mean, *was*?" A flicker of surprised hurt shattered Randy's carefree laughter.

"I mean exactly what I said."

Randy sat up, suddenly somber. "You're saying this because I'm leaving, not because you mean it." His voice was steady and slow like someone clarifying instructions given in a foreign language.

The blood rushed to Meg's cheeks. She was no longer a yellow rose wilting, but a steaming kettle. Her words spat out hot and fast. "No, I'm not saying this because you're leaving. I'm saying this because it's true." She stood up. Chair legs scraping floor. "I don't know why I've put up with your childish nonsense all these years. I was stupid to think you'd outgrow it. That you were capable of that much."

"Meg, pleeease." Randy swiveled out of his chair and knelt on the tile floor. He clasped his hands, a pleading lover. "Say you won't leave me, baby." Meg stalked down the aisle. Her heels clip-clopped on the tiles. Randy cupped his hands around his mouth. "I'll marry you, if that's what you want." Meg squeezed between two waitresses and turned the corner, not even glancing back.

Randy stared forlornly at where Meg had stood, but made no effort to chase her. Instead, he uncurled his spine and lifted himself to his feet. He looked taller than six feet, pitifully gaunt, and ironically dignified. He erected his toppled over chair and slumped heavily into the vinyl seat. "I don't know what she's so angry about. I told her she could come surf the waves with me," he said. He raised his empty glass. A thin brown streak moved from one end of the glass to the other. "You're lucky, Howie.

Your woman let's you do anything. Isn't that right, Jude?"

He's right, I thought. I had let Howard do whatever he wanted. When he decided to manage the *White Demons*, I let him. When he changed his mind and accepted a job as a network specialist, I let him. When he found out I was unexpectedly pregnant, and he confessed to me his desire to be a parent, I let him. I let him do anything.

Randy glanced up. Our eyes locked and I wondered what he was thinking. An uncomfortable silence stitched between us. "You know, I was only kidding about the touchdown. I mean, if it offended you, I'm sorry. Really, I am. I only want what's best for the little bambino, I mean, baby." His eyes, crazy eyes, one green, the other slightly yellow, stared at me like they wanted to press on through to the other side. I didn't know what to say. This was not the Randy I cherished, the Randy who did not know how to be serious, and for a moment, I thought I had lost him. Then he lifted his glass and slammed it down. "Oh, hell. I'm better off without her. Damn bitch."

"Enough," Howard said.

Randy scowled at him, then me. "I suppose you both feel the same way about me, but haven't had the courage to say it, huh?"

Howard's jaw tensed. He motioned as if he might reach across the table and restrain Randy, which would be a first, but he didn't.

Randy glanced at me. "I'm sorry," he said.

"It's okay." I placed my fingers over his wrist, tentatively, feeling the coolness of his skin. His gaze covered my hand. I was surprised he didn't pull away.

"We'll miss you," I said.

"That's nice of you to say, but if it's not true, then why bother?"

"I mean it, I really do." He pulled his hand away. "Listen, no one sings like you do or plays the drums with such passion." I felt my voice faltering in my throat. I spoke fast, faster, hoping the words would mask the trembling fear and urgency to make him understand how much I cared. "Who will call out to me across a parking lot, 'Hey, Jude,' and when I call back, 'Sing it, Paul', break into a croon? Who will I go to when I need a piece of music trivia? Who will I talk to when I desperately need to laugh and have some fun?"

"You've got Howie. What more could you want?"

You, I thought. Your crooked smile, your way of seeing things upside down, inside out, the way you can turn everything into a joke, even if it's life-threatening or sorrowful. But I didn't say it, because Howard was sitting with us, listening, and I felt I'd already said too much. And Randy, probably thinking he had made his point clear, heaved a sigh.

"I think I'll go get another drink," Randy said. He stood up, slouched at the shoulders, thin and defeated. "Anyone want anything?"

We both shook our heads, though I could have used a shot of tequila.

"All right," Randy said. The waitress set a platter of food on a folding tray. "Go ahead and eat. I don't know how long I'll be."

The waitress smiled, befuddled and polite, not wanting to inquire about the absence of two members, but curious nonetheless. She appeared to be relatively new and I supposed she was wondering if the hostility sparking the air had anything to do with her service.

"Can I get you anything?" she asked, ready to grab the notepad and pencil in her apron pocket.

"No, thank you. We're fine," Howard said. The waitress nodded, not sure if she did the right thing or not, and moved to the next table.

"Are you all right?" Howard asked me.

I shrugged. The baby rolled over and over, again and again, heedless of the disturbances outside.

"You look a little piqued. Maybe you should go to the restroom and freshen up and check on Meg while you're there."

"Only if you check on Randy?" I flashed.

Howard grimaced. "He's probably drunk by now."

"I know. That's why I want you to check on him."

In the restroom, Meg splashed her face with water and touched up her hair. When she saw me, the anger returned to her eyes.

"I suppose he sent you to come fetch me," Meg said.

"Howard did."

Meg's anger flared, then died. Apparently, she could forgive Howard's gesture of kindness. Then, matter-of-factly, Meg added, "I bet Randy's at the bar."

"How did you guess?" I gazed at myself in the mirror. The skin around my eyes was tired and puffy.

"I'm sorry for losing control." Meg withdrew a small brush and fluffed her blond waves. "It's just that I can't take it anymore. He never thinks about me. It's always himself or his interests. You know, the night he told you about the fellowship to Bali was the first time I had heard of it. We've been together for eight years and you'd think he'd have the common courtesy to tell me. I know we're not married, but even so, I am entitled to something, am I not?"

"Of course, you are." I imagined Randy had applied for the fellowship on a whim, never thinking he'd actually be accepted, and when he was, I'm sure he was just as surprised as the rest of us were. "I don't think he kept it a secret to hurt you."

"That's just it. He doesn't realize there are consequences to his actions. At least, Howard has some common sense."

"Were you serious about it being over with Randy?"

Meg shoved her brush in her purse and snapped it shut. Her eyes were a calm gray-blue. "It's time to move on. I would have done it sooner, if I had known he was never going to grow up, change, become successful. Like Howard."

I wrapped my arms around Meg. Her slender body pressed against the weight around my stomach. "Oh, Judy, you're so lucky. You have Howard, and the baby. I have nothing."

I wanted to tell Meg being married and pregnant was not as glamorous as she imagined it to be, that Howard had wanted the child, not me, that I would rather Randy had asked me to come join him, surfing the waves half a world away, and not Meg. I wanted to tell Meg how I envied her freedom, the liberty Randy had given her all those years, never tying her down to a decision, letting her change her mind if she wanted to. It didn't matter if she wanted things he couldn't give her. Randy had always made it clear she was free to go somewhere else. I wanted to tell her about the pain I was in, knowing in weeks my life would change forever. I couldn't just pick up and go whenever I liked, and no matter how much Howard helped, no matter how good a father he chose to be, I'd be the one who had to tailor my life to fit the newborn's schedule, even after I returned to checking facts for a third-rate magazine. But I didn't know how to make her understand how lonely I was losing who I imagined myself to be a writer, a lover, a friend, and how used I felt with my skin stretched beyond believable proportions, my nights occupied with indigestion and my days spaced out between trips to the restroom and cravings for food I wouldn't normally eat. Randy would go, come back, and Meg could go on with or without him. She had a choice. I had already chosen, and my decision was not on a whim, not for a year, but deliberate and for a lifetime. Couldn't she see that?

"Why don't you and Howard take Randy to the airport? I'm driving home." She pulled away, straightened her dress. The scalloped neckline showcased her gently defined collar bones. "I'll call you when I get in." Meg hugged me briefly, then let go. "Talk to Randy for me. I don't intend on speaking to him again."

I waddled out of the restroom. Even from a distance, I could see

Howard sitting alone at our table, munching on a steak and chicken fajita, sneaking a fry from my plate. I assumed either he hadn't talked to Randy or Randy didn't want to talk to him.

I shuffled into the dimly lit bar. Everyone turned to stare at me, questioning the appropriateness of my being there as if I didn't have the sense enough to not drink being this pregnant. I ignored the stares, even though I felt them burn through me, and sidled up to Randy who was slumped over the counter nursing a double vodka. I touched his arm.

"Hey, Jude."

For the first time, I didn't say, "Sing it, Paul."

He glanced at the flickering images of the TV, downed the liquor, and flagged the bartender for another.

"Here, have a seat." He moved over to the next bar stool. "I already talked to Howie. He says I should apologize to Meg."

"Meg said it's over."

"Just as well." He downed the next drink.

"I don't suppose you'll write?"

"Why should I? It's over."

"Not to her. To us. To Howard and me and the baby."

"Yeah. Sure."

But I knew Randy. He'd send a postcard when he arrived, terrified and thrilled to be there, and then shortly after the baby was born—three, maybe six months later—the letters would stop and we'd never know whether or not he was back in the States.

I didn't suppose there was any point in trying to get him to understand me. What did I have to say that couldn't be said before? That I cared? That I'd miss him? That I thought he might have understood me when I felt no one else did? No, it was too late for explanations. My stomach growled. My hamburger and fries were getting cold.

I turned around when I felt his hand on my shoulder. He slipped off the bar stool and I had to catch him. He bumped into my stomach and the baby kicked him. He laughed, cupping my face with his palms, and kissed me. It was a reckless kiss, wet and sloppy. His lips slipped across my mouth and chin.

I pulled away, appalled by his ignorant selfishness.

"Hey, Jude, don't go. I just lost Meggy." He gripped my shoulders and began to lead me in a two-step. He sung, soft and low, into my ear. It took me a moment to realize he was singing, "Angels in Underwear." I closed my eyes, hypnotized by his voice, throaty and clear, in spite of the liquor. I felt the years unravel and unite. Randy was not part of the past, and the baby did not exist only in the future. With Randy's long slim hands on my shoulders, his warm breath against my cheek, his knobby knees hitting my thighs, my back nudging into strangers, and the baby rolling around in soft waves inside of me, I shifted my weight from foot to foot keeping time with Randy's lead, back and forth, back and forth. The room seemed to lose its walls and we danced through a space defined only by the rhythm of our heartbeats, all three of us—Randy, the baby, and I—delightfully out of sync.

Lips

I was here. That's what she means when she writes in big block letters with her bright red lipstick, TYC 2001, in the mirror of the girls' bathroom in Jefferson High School.

I stand beside her pretending to fluff my already exaggerated hairdo. She thinks I don't know her importance so she draws a line beneath her initials with a sweep of her wrist.

TYC catches me staring at her. "What you looking at?" She narrows her brown eyes, swivels the lipstick into its black case, turns, and struts away. TYC is not like my best friend, Lorraine, who moved to Arizona last summer when she was just three days shy of turning sixteen. I try hard not to think of Lorraine. She's there and I'm here. And here is where I want to stay.

The bell rings for third period. I have history. So does TYC. She's in my class and sits in the back row. Her backpack is full of notebooks she never uses and a sweatshirt she never wears. On her neck, a silver chain holds the key to her house on Fourth Street, two blocks from the 7-Eleven, where I once spotted her while I was buying a Slurpee. She didn't say hello, just glared at me with her *how-dare-you* frown as she pushed past the construction worker in a cowboy hat buying a hot dog to lean across the counter shoving her cleavage in the face of a nineteen-year-old pimple-faced clerk and demanding a pack of Marlboro Lights. The dumbfounded clerk handed them to her without checking I.D. To make things worse, he forgot to ring up the sale. TYC lit a cigarette before leaving the store and smoked two more before turning the key to her front door.

When the second bell rings, I'm sitting in the front row beside Suki who always turns in completed homework assignments and scores 92% or higher on every test. Suki bows her dark head above her open book and takes notes even when Miss Wilson isn't talking. I try to pretend I'm just as studious. In the margin of my notebook, I draw TYC's lips and color them in with my pencil. In art, I'll magnify those lips one hundred times and shade them with pastels. Mr. Carpenter, the art instructor, will tell me I'm as bold as Picasso, painting in colors that don't normally appear on lips, like, emerald green, turquoise and lemon yellow.

By the time school lets out at three-thirty, I've seen TYC three more times: by the lockers exchanging her history book for algebra; in the halls shouting at a cheerleader for accidentally touching her; and, the library checking out a book written by Dorothy Allison.

I start to think there's more to my fascination with TYC than her bright red lipstick, which she never wears, only writes with. At home, I stare in the mirror at my reflection and pucker my lips and mouth the letters, TYC, like I'm some sort of rock star in a music video. Before I go to sleep, I sit on the edge of my bed and roll up my pajama sleeves and stare at my wrists, turning them from side to side. The bones are heavy and awkward, not slim and manipulative. I lie down and pull the covers toward my chin. I close my eyes and dream of large techno-colored lips. I wake up in the middle of the night and feel my heart racing. I touch my lips with the tips of my fingers, the same lips those large techno-colored lips just kissed.

***

The next day I bring my lunch: a very small bologna sandwich and an extra tall thermos of lemonade. I climb the steps of the outdoor auditorium and sit next to TYC who studies a coin-size hole in the knee of her jeans like she's looking through a microscope. The air is crisp and clear. The laughter and chatter of the cafeteria hardly reaches up these steps and I begin to understand why TYC eats her lunch up here. It's almost quiet like church. The distant hum of the other students sounds like a hymn, reverential and holy. I bite into the sandwich and wash it down with lemonade.

Beside me, TYC chomps on her Mexican pizza. The crisp tortilla crunches against her molars. She sips Diet Coke. In the sunlight, the roots of her kinky black hair are copper and wiry. She squints and stares off across campus. I wonder what she's thinking.

Then she turns and our eyes meet. I feel a jolt of discovery power through me and I tremble. "What you looking at?" TYC asks, glaring at me.

I crumple the plastic bag with my half-eaten sandwich and shove it into my backpack. Unsure of what to say, I stand up to leave.

"Scaredy cat," she taunts.

I don't say anything as I bound down the steps without stopping to tie my unlaced shoe or daring to look back.

***

My bedroom is a haven. After school, I close the door and pull the curtains shut and curl up on my quilt comforter with my bare feet tucked under my hips. I flip through my mother's magazines, *Redbook* and *Vogue*, which she writes off as business expenses for her salon. Unlike my mother, I could care less about the hairstyles and fashions. I read the articles on sex and romance, health and fitness, time management and stress relief. When I get bored, I pull out my sketchpad and draw until the sun sets and it's time to eat. In the evenings, after homework, I pour a handful of beads into the palm of my hand and count backwards from 100. These are Lorraine's beads, which she used to make into beautiful necklaces and sell at the local flee market. When her father got a job transfer, she gave me the beads as a going away present. In her big, loopy scrawl, she wrote, "I love you," in a farewell card. In return, I gave her Sunshine, the stuffed bear I had since preschool, and a card with a kitten holding a broken heart. Inside I wrote, "K.I.T. I'll miss you." Three weeks after she moved, Lorraine sent me a postcard of the desert and a brief note: "It's HOT." I wrote her back instantly. A month later, after writing again and receiving no response, I started to lose hope.

"She's probably busy making new friends," my mother said to comfort me.

Although it may have been true, I didn't want to think about it. I couldn't imagine Lorraine's life without me.

In the stillness, my thoughts circle from Lorraine's parting gift to TYC's unforgiving glare. I squint into my makeup mirror and practice looking fierce. It's no use. My face, to quote my father, is too plain to be obnoxious. I tease my hair with my fingers and get ready for bed, spilling the beads back into their plastic vial, tucking it between my mattresses along with Lorraine's card.

In the dark, I try to sleep but not to dream.

***

"Why you following me?" TYC spins around and eyes me up and down.

It's been two weeks since I first noticed her bright red lipstick on the mirror in this restroom. I hold my breath and count to three, wondering why I feel compelled to offer an explanation. "I have to pee."

"No way. You following me."

Her brown eyes flash with anger. A stall becomes available and the girl behind us asks if she can use it first, since it looks like we're busy. TYC frowns. "No way."

Before TYC enters the stall, she warns, "Don't leave. I want talk to you."

My stomach twirls. My palms sweat. I fumble with the paper liner for the toilet seat. My zipper catches. My heart beat pounds inside my chest. For a moment, I think I will die.

She stands in front of the two sinks with her bright red lipstick poised above the mirror. I think she's going to write her initials, but she writes something else instead. It is a poem.

Roses are red.

Violets are blue.

Sugar is sweet

And I hate you.

The water is cool against my hands. There is no paper towel in the dispenser. I dry my palms against my jeans and try to avoid TYC's insolent glower.

She tucks her lipstick inside her backpack and turns to me. "You a spy?"

"No," I say.

"Then why you following me?"

"I'm not following you."

"Yes, you are. I seen you. In the library. During break. During lunch. After school. You're always there. What you want with me?"

I feel my heart stutter as my mouth opens wide. "I want to hang out with you."

TYC grabs my "Love Is Color Blind" T-shirt and pulls me toward her, just inches from her thick, pouty lips. Her breath is hot and moist against my skin. "Don't follow me," she warns. "I don't have friends. I don't need friends."

I nod, pretending to understand, but all I see are her lips—full, luscious lips that barely move. I hold my breath and feel my chest contract with fear and longing.

I wait and wait and wait.

She stares at me with her dense brown eyes, all that careless hatred boiling like a cauldron beneath her cocoa butter skin. For a moment, I think she will hit me, knock me unconscious, or at least, baffle me with her boyish arrogance. But she lets me go, and I slump against the cool wall.

She turns around and swings her backpack over her shoulder. The lipstick falls out of the unzipped pocket and rolls across the stained linoleum. I bend to pick it up. My outstretched arm reaches toward her, my voice calling, "You dropped something."

But she's gone. I stare at the tube of bright red lipstick and resist the impulse to chase her.

***

The next day at school I keep my distance. I don't look. I don't follow. I pretend TYC no longer exists.

In history, to abate the growing loneliness, I ask Suki if we can study for the next exam together. She smiles. Her eyes slant into almonds. We meet at the library during lunch. Suki bends her head and whispers under the curtain of her black hair. I write down everything she says, word for word, as if she is giving me the ingredients to a secret potion. We exchange phone numbers and promise to call to get together over the weekend to quiz each other.

At home, after dinner, I undress and crawl into bed. Reaching between mattresses, I remove Lorraine's card and beads and throw them into the wastebasket beside my desk. When I'm done, I grab the lipstick off the nightstand, twist the tube and rub bright red paint in bold curves over my thin lips. I kiss the back of my hand the way Lorraine used to when we were practicing how to kiss boys. At fourteen, Lorraine got her first boyfriend. She told me everything about what he liked to do to her and what she liked to do to him that I felt awkward seeing them together.

"How does it feel to be kissed?" I asked her once, during a sleepover.

Without a word, she pulled me close and pressed her lips against my teeth until I felt her tongue in my mouth, strangely soft and moist and warm.

The Human Act

I see her feet first. White Reeboks, size 7 ½, with mud on the soles coming straight at me. Then I look up past the knotty sinews of her legs in denim shorts, past the belly button and small, swinging breasts in a white cut-off T-shirt, past her narrow chin and high ruddy cheekbones to her deep-set brown eyes full of tenderness and love. I'm so lost admiring those sad and hopeful eyes that I don't notice her left arm winding up a pitch until she says, "Go fetch it, Marcus."

I stagger to the left through choppy grass, scampering over beetles and ladybugs' nests, trying desperately to beat the breath of a late spring breeze that exhales the softball Amelia has thrown toward me. I move a little more to the left, then forward, then step back a few paces, then stop, rise up on my hind legs, open my mouth and lean forward. Got it! The gummy material bounces against my teeth and then mysteriously falls away. Oh, no!

"Better luck next time," Amelia says, jogging toward me and bending over to retrieve the soppy softball. With her free hand she rubs behind my ears and under my chin. I close my eyes and luxuriate in the gentle love of her massage. When she stops, I start to whimper. She palms the softball, wiping my slobber against her denim shorts, and smiles. "Want to try again?"

I bark enthusiastically, though I don't really feel like it. All I can hear in my head is her boyfriend, Phil, saying what he always says when I'm around, "You can't teach an old dog new tricks."

I am seven years old. Five of those years I spent on the streets. I had a family once, when I was a puppy, but it didn't last for long. I couldn't follow the rules:

Don't sit on the sofa.

Don't pee in the house.

Don't jump on anyone.

For a while, I was moved from shelter to home, home to shelter, then I escaped and traveled the back alleys, rummaging through garbage cans. I know what it feels like to be cold and homeless.

Then I met Amelia.

She was coming home from work at the legal office where she represents corporations in billion dollar mergers. She bent over the trunk of her gray Volvo and removed a single bag of groceries. With a grace both astonishingly simple and stunningly learned, she closed the trunk with her elbow and proceeded to balance the groceries against one hip while humming a tune.

Eager for a look at her face, I stepped in front of her. She tripped on my front paws and staggered back, regaining her balance. Shock and fear melted into kindness and concern. She stooped to examine me, setting her groceries on the lower step. "You look hungry," she said, combing her fingers through my matted fur. "And lonely." Her face was fuller then, with softly rounded cheeks and a subtle double chin. She gathered me into her arms and I licked her neck helplessly. Then she screeched and shoved me out of her lap, standing up and glancing down at her black slacks drenched in pee. I thought for certain I had blown it, but she just shook her head and wiped her pants with a tissue from her purse. "We'll have to fix that," she said, stooping to gather her groceries. "Come on, let's get something to eat."

I trotted behind her up the stairs and down the hall to her one bedroom apartment. She once again perched the groceries against her hip while fumbling with a jangling set of keys on a long golden key chain with a picture of the sun dipping into the Pacific. She threw open the door and invited me into her spacious living room with its neutral carpet and eggshell walls. I trotted past the built-in bookcases lining either side of a marble fireplace to the loveseat and sofa across from the sliding glass door that lead to the small yard that would become my sometimes home, sometimes prison.

While Amelia stocked fresh fruits and vegetables in the crisper, I sniffed my reflection in the glass coffee table that was trimmed with oak. A row of photographs of her family graced the end tables and the bookshelves. I noticed a brother and a sister, a mother and a father, and someone else, someone special. His photograph pierced the center of a stainless steel heart. With windswept sandy blond curls and rugged mountain climbing muscles, he seemed unusually turbulent, even with a cloudless smile, and some part of me knew, instinctively, that I would have to battle him to retain a space in Amelia's otherwise rambling, open field heart.

Amelia smiles, not sensing how hard I am trying to please her. She winds up another pitch and asks, "Are you ready?"

I bark and leap into the air. I'd do anything for Amelia. Anything. Even slop around in a muddy soccer field chasing fly balls, trying to catch them in my small mouth and bring them back to her like ten-carat diamonds dug up from the depths of my hound-dog heart.

When we get home, Phil is sitting on the sofa. He has a key to the apartment that he uses when Amelia's out of town on business and someone needs to care for me. On the coffee table, the morning classifieds and sports sections litter the glass. When Amelia opens the closet to hang up her sweater, two suitcases topple out.

"Cece's leaving me," Phil says. "I thought I could stay here."

Amelia's lips tighten. "Can you go home and talk about it? I thought you were seeing a counselor?"

"We were. She told the counselor last night that she wants a divorce. She says she's found someone who listens."

Amelia unlaces her Reeboks and sets the softball inside the left shoe. She runs her fingers through her long brown hair and tries to smile. I'm thirsty from chasing muddy softballs, so I trot into the kitchen and lap up the clean water Amelia placed there this morning after we had breakfast. When Phil's here, the rooms feel smaller, darker, cluttered. I stay in the kitchen, chewing Purina dog chow, eyeing Amelia in the living room. She curls up beside Phil on the loveseat and brushes a sandy curl off his forehead.

"I guess it will be all right. You can probably find a place by the end of the month."

Phil kisses her mouth. "What would I do without you?"

By the end of the month, I've given up my space in Amelia's bed to Phil. I sleep outside, eat outside, and pee outside. My chewy toys no longer hide beneath the sofa cushions or underneath the coffee table. The apartment is still a mess, but it's a different kind of mess. Phil's Polo shirts drape over the sofa's arms. On an end table where Amelia's reading lamp used to be, a portable television blasts a baseball game between the Yankees and the Dodgers. Monitors and hardware cases lean like Lego cities on either side of the fireplace. Sometimes Phil thinks he's home and he trips on my paws or steps on my tail. I yelp. Amelia says, "Be careful," but doesn't do anything when he's not. I'm beginning to wonder when they're going to send me away like the last family did a month after they brought a new baby home. "There just isn't enough room in this house for another mouth to feed," the husband said. I thought they'd get rid of the baby, he came last, after all, but they got rid of me.

Amelia isn't holding up any better. She's lost a lot of weight. When she bends down to feed or pet me, I can see each bone in her wrists. And her sad smile.

Five weeks later, Phil says he's finally found a place. I think we ought to celebrate. But the night before he's supposed to move out, Amelia closes a deal between Soltech and Fusetronics and, in the process of restructuring, Phil loses his job as a software engineer.

Phil slams the door when he comes home. Amelia is cooking in the kitchen, dicing onions for the soup she will not eat. I am sitting by her feet, just happy to be near her.

"How could you?" Phil spits. "I may not love my kids as much as you love that damn dog, but at least my kids would never back stab me."

Veiled by her hair, Amelia continues dicing. "You knew I was working on that deal long before it became final. If you had a problem with it, you should have said something then."

Phil stalks into the kitchen and kicks over my water bowl and steps into the moist crumbs of dog chow. "Shit. His crap is everywhere. I thought I told you to keep it outside where it belongs."

"We had a snack together. Is that so horrible?"

"You could at least get rid of the evidence." Phil dumps the bowl of water in the sink and rinses the dog chow down the drain. He mops the floor. He pulls open the refrigerator and moves around my cans of moist dog food looking for a beer. "You know, the Italian Affair is having its grand opening tonight. We should go there and celebrate your big deal."

"Stop teasing me. It *was* a big deal negotiating that offer. I couldn't write in the terms and conditions for everything. How could I have known they would lay you off?"

I whine and whimper, hoping Amelia will understand. *Please, don't let him stay.*

But she's not paying attention to me. She's paying attention to him. "Listen, Phil,

I'm sorry. If it makes you feel better, you can stay here until you get another job."

Phil pops the lid on a can of beer. Foam rises over the edge. He slurps it up and wipes froth off his mouth with the back of his hand. "I'm sorry, too. It's just that most guys my age are settling down, not starting over."

Amelia touches his cheek. "Beginnings aren't bad. They're endings upside down. Like a frown to a smile. You have to look at it the right way. Now you have time to do the things you've always wanted to do. Like play softball."

"You're right." Phil wraps his arms around her waist and kisses her. "It's not all bad."

***

It's not all good, either. During the next month, Amelia stops eating breakfast and only picks at the elaborate dinners she prepares for Phil. Chilled avocado soup, gazpacho salad, broccoli rabe soufflé, and orange tuiles for desert. At night, after Phil has fallen asleep, she slips out into the living room and unlatches the sliding glass door and whispers, "Marcus. Marcus, come in."

I nestle in her lap while she reads from one of the many books she has purchased over the last two weeks: *Women Who Love Too Much. Feeding the Hungry Heart. The Verbally Abusive Relationship. Should You Leave?*

Sometimes she reads a particular passage out loud and asks for my opinion. If I bark too loudly, Phil tosses awake and patters out into the living room in his navy robe and asks what is she doing up and what for god's sake am I doing inside. I growl at Phil. When Amelia refuses to send me outside, Phil slaps my back and shouts, "Bad dog." I dart into my prison.

Amelia shoves the books into a kitchen cupboard where she keeps laxatives and a box of See's candy, soft-centers, which she sometimes shares with me in spite of the vet's reprimand about how chocolate ruins my digestion. Then, she locks herself in the bathroom and cries until Phil beats on the door and tells her to come out.

"You're worse than my kids. Tell me what's wrong with you?"

From behind the door, her voice seems diminished even though she's shouting. "I don't like living this way. It's not what I had in mind when I started this relationship."

Phil says, "You don't love me anymore."

"Of course, I do. It has nothing to do with love. I just want to be free to live my own life according to my own rules. I don't want you telling me when to go to bed and when to put Marcus out. You understand?"

"No, *you* don't understand. I don't want dog dander in my hair when I wake up in the morning. No matter how much you wash, you can't get that sewer smell out of your skin. I don't understand why you just didn't bring him to the pound when you found him. You don't need a dog for a companion. You have me."

"Sometimes I think having you is worse than having a dog."

"Oh, yeah? Well, at least I know how to sit at a table and eat politely and clean up after I'm done. I don't pee all over your new Persian rug or knock over the vase I bought you because I am glad you're finally home. I don't bark at all hours of the day and night and annoy the neighbors. I don't ask you to clean my poop or take me for a walk or bathe or feed me. I do the human act pretty well."

"So well so your wife kicked you out and won't let you have custody over the two human beings you helped bring into this world."

"Shut up! You don't know anything about my marriage or my family."

"Of course I don't. You never shared any of that part of your life with me."

"How could I? I was having an affair. You're supposed to keep secrets."

"From your wife and your kids, maybe. But not from me."

"What makes you so special?"

"Because I want to be with you. Not out of obligation or duty, but out of love. Pure and simple love."

"Nothing is ever pure and simple. Especially not love."

Phil slips on a pair of slacks, shoes, throws on a shirt, grabs his keys and slams the front door. A few minutes later, water runs in the bathroom and the toilet flushes several times. Amelia unlocks the door and stumbles out looking weak and pale. She unlatches the sliding glass door and lets me in. I follow her into the kitchen where she devours a pint of vanilla ice cream, then pours herself a glass of water and swallows twelve laxatives. She opens the refrigerator and stares at the leftovers in their Tupperware containers and then shuts the door. From beneath the sink, she dumps dog chow into the empty ice cream container and sets it beside a fresh bowl of water. She slumps down beside me as I eat. The ends of her hair break off into her hands when she twirls them away from her face. She buries her head against her knees and starts sobbing again.

I stop eating and nuzzle my cold wet nose against her elbow. She sits up momentarily and gathers me into her arms. "You understand me, don't you, Marcus? I want to have a little control over my life again. That isn't too much to ask for, is it?"

I whine and whimper, offering my sympathy. Amelia rubs her nose against my nose. I lick her ice cream mouth until she breaks into a smile. I want her to know I would do anything to make her happy. Anything.

***

Things seem to be getting better. Phil joins a softball team, the Mad Monsters, and leaves three nights a week for practice. Amelia and I treasure our nights alone. We curl up on the sofa and watch old black and white Lassie movies. Sometimes we share popcorn, though I'd rather have chocolate. The kernels stick between my teeth and sometimes I swallow them and choke. Amelia says, "Poor baby," and sets a bowl of water on the coffee table for me. I lap it up, watching her, watching the television, watching the front door, waiting for Phil's keys to jangle and signal my return to the glass prison.

Although her diet doesn't change, Amelia starts jogging with me every morning before work. On weekends when Phil has a game, she takes me to the park and we practice catching softballs. I enjoy my time with her, alone, although I still don't care too much for fetching. By mid-afternoon we come home, dirty and happy. When Phil arrives, Amelia greets him with wide arms and passionate kisses. I bark and leap for a hug. Phil gets down on his knees and rubs my belly until I can't stand it anymore and I have to pee. Phil snaps, "Bad dog," then sends me out into the glass cage. Amelia winks, and I know I won't be exiled for the night.

Sometimes Phil wrestles Amelia to the floor. He rolls around in his muddy uniform grinding stains into the white carpet and into her T-shirt. Amelia doesn't say, "Bad man," and send him to the bathroom to clean up. She giggles with pleasure and playfully says, "Stop it. You're worse than Marcus," jabbing him with her gaunt elbows. Phil barks and licks her hollow cheeks and sharp chin and buries his sweaty head between her breasts.

After they tumble around and make love, Amelia unlatches the door and lets me in while Phil showers and changes. She gets down on her hands and knees and scrubs the stains from the carpet. I lope into the kitchen and gnaw on a bone from last night's dinner.

On Saturday, after Phil hits a home run and the Mad Monsters win, we celebrate.

Amelia rents a boat on Lake Elizabeth. One of Phil's teammates takes our picture while we're on deck, squinting in the early summer sun. Amelia and Phil wrap their arms around each other and lean close to me. Everything feels perfect.

A week later when Amelia picks up the photos, we discover the picture is ruined.

Someone exposed the film before it was developed. A dark shadow eclipses our faces. Amelia scours the house looking for the receipt so she can return the wooden picture frame she bought etched with the words, "Family." Phil tries to reason with her, telling her there will be other pictures, better ones that she can put in there. But Amelia decides to return the frame. "I couldn't stand looking at it empty like that," she says.

***

This morning Amelia and I jog down to the park. Sunlight peaks over the horizon and breaks through the trees, flashing against her glistening skin and my matted fur. The concrete starts to warm beneath my paws. Amelia's breaths get shorter and shorter, sharpen into pants, then gasps. She slows down. I trip on her ankles and yelp. She flops forward from the waist, her long hair touching the cement. I bark for help. She slumps to her knees, then rocks back on her heels and pushes the hair from her face. Her lips swell blue. I break free from the leash and trot over to another jogger, a man with wind-blown hair and a green windbreaker. *Help! Help!* I bark, leaping and pawing his legs. The man glances down and follows me to where Amelia lays.

He squats and feels her neck for a pulse. He frowns, then reaches into his pocket and withdraws a cell phone. "Hello, I need an ambulance. There's a woman unconscious. We're at Springfield Park. Please, hurry."

I nuzzle up against Amelia's neck and lick her cheeks and her blue lips, but she doesn't move. Curling up beside her, I whimper and worry. The male jogger strokes my head. "She'll be all right, sport. We're getting help. You're a good dog for getting me. She's lucky to have you."

When the paramedics arrive, they won't let me ride with them to the hospital. The male jogger asks if we can follow in his BMW. They agree. Riding beside the male jogger on black leather upholstery, I try my hardest to contain my anxiety. But I can't. A stream of pee puddles under me. The male jogger nods. "You must really love her," he says, in a calm and even voice.

I wag my tail and bark. I would do anything for my Amelia. Anything.

***

The doctor says Amelia will be all right. "She's severely dehydrated and malnourished. We'll be keeping her overnight for observation."

Phil receives a call at home and meets us outside the emergency room. The male jogger informs him about the situation and Phil glances down at me without a smile. "Thanks for your help. I'll take things from here."

The male jogger nods. "Let me say good-bye, first." He bends down and rubs me under the chin. "You're a good dog. Remember that." The sliding glass doors part and the male jogger strolls into the emergency room to visit Amelia.

When we're alone, Phil kicks the curb. "She wasn't eating? My god, there's never food in the house. Why didn't you say something?"

I cower near the bushes. *What would I have told him?* That between fasts Amelia ate mouthful after mouthful of Dreyer's vanilla ice cream and swallowed handfuls of pink laxatives. That after their fights and while he was out looking for work, Amelia would binge on anything she found in the cupboards and in the refrigerator, sometimes chewing on my dog food when everything else was gone. Immediately afterward, she would lock herself in the bathroom and run the water and flush the toilet and emerge an hour later looking pale and weak. That she would wake up night after night restless and worried and cuddle with me on the sofa reading self-help books that only made her feel worse. That when she talked about Phil it was always in reference to the life he had left, to the two boys he had abandoned, to the wife he had once spoken fondly of whenever he had a chance. That she was tired of the demands of keeping a home for a man she only wanted to have around once in a while, not all the time, she sometimes wanted to be able to put him in the glass prison and stretch out on her big bed with me or alone. And how she wanted, more than anything, to love and to be loved. That's all, I bark. Is that too much to ask?

"Shut up!" Phil screams. I hush. For a moment, Phil reels around as if looking for something to kick, but then he changes his mind and sits down on the curb and buries his head in his hands and starts sobbing. Surprised, I lift my ears. "My god, my god, my god," he mumbles. "I'm so damn caught up in myself I didn't even notice she was crying out for help."

I curl up beside him and listen.

"I know it's hard to believe, but before you came along Amelia and I were happy." He lifts his head and his eyes are red and his skin is blotchy. "It was a whole lot easier when I could say goodnight and go home and spend time with my family. I miss helping Tyler with decimals. I miss reading *Goodnight Moon* to Scott. I even miss fighting with Cece. I miss the way she would thrust her lower lip and pout when I said I was too tired for anything. It was the truth. I would fall asleep on the sofa while she was playing with my hair and telling me about the cute things the boys said when she picked them up from school. I miss my old life."

I lay a paw on his arm.

He pats my head. "I never thought it would come to this."

***

The next day, the doctor releases Amelia with a prescription for antidepressants and appointments to see a nutritionist and a psychologist for a thorough evaluation. I've been good all day, staying on the patio, not barking, peeing where I'm supposed to, so Phil relents and lets me come with him to pick her up. I sit in the backseat and press my nose against the window. Phil plays the radio softly and drums his fingers against the steering wheel. When Amelia slips into the front seat, I jump and paw her hair. She turns to me and smiles. "You saved my life, Marcus."

I bark and wag my tail and pee all over the backseat.

For the first time, Phil doesn't yell at me. He is quiet as he drives. Then, a few minutes later, at a stop light, Phil says to Amelia, "You didn't tell me you had a problem with food."

Amelia leans her head against the seat and stares out the side window. "You've kept secrets all your life, Phil. From your wife. From your kids. What difference does it make if I kept one little secret for me?"

"This is different."

"How so? Because it doesn't require high attorney's fees?"

Phil turns down a street lined with oaks and houses, the kind of place with fenced lawns where children play, a place where I once lived. He parks and turns to face Amelia. But she doesn't want to look at him. She gazes out the window at a child playing catch with his terrier. There are tears in her eyes that dance, but do not fall. Phil touches her shoulder. She winces.

"Listen. This isn't about the divorce. It's about you. Your health. The nurse explained to me how much weight you've lost. You know, I didn't think anything of it—women are always dieting. I chalked it up to stress. But the nurse said you could've died." Phil squeezes her hands. "I don't want to lose you."

Amelia sniffles. Tears stream down her cheeks. She doesn't turn to face him, but stares out the side window at the terrier as he dashes across the lawn, chasing the softball, bringing it back to the boy who rubs behind his ears and throws the ball again. When she speaks, her voice is soft and quiet, almost gentle. "You've already lost me."

***

Phil starts looking for an apartment. On the weekends, Amelia joins him. When they're together, they talk like good friends. Phil asks about

Amelia's new clients, her visits to the nutritionist and the psychologist, her weekly support group. She tells him someone calls her every night, before and after dinner, to make sure she's eating something healthy like a banana or a potato and keeping it down. Phil tells her about a job opening at a small software firm downtown, and how the boys would like to spend half their weeks with him if he can find a place close to school.

By the first of August, Phil gets a job and moves into a two-bedroom apartment across from Cedar Elementary. At first, Phil calls Amelia once a week to check up on her, but gradually, the phone calls become less and less frequent. By the end of September, Phil stops calling.

One night, in early October, Amelia opens a can of moist dog food and scrapes it into a clean bowl. She sets it along with a bowl of water on the kitchen table and pulls back a chair. I leap up and sit next to her and wait while she lights candles and says grace. In the flickering light and shadows, she chews her salad while I chomp on ground beef. She doesn't tell me to eat quietly or to close my mouth when I chew. When the phone rings, she answers it.

At first, I think it's a woman from her support group. But her eyebrows lift in surprise and a smile steals across her face. "Oh my god, I thought I'd never hear from you again," she says. Then, covering the mouthpiece of the phone, she leans over and whispers, "It's the jogger who called the ambulance." I bark and wag my tail, *Can I talk to him?*

Amelia says, "Wait, I have an old friend who wants to say hello." She places the receiver against my mouth and I bark.

The male jogger laughs. "Good to hear from you, sport," he says. "Would it be all right if I asked your woman out?"

I bark again and he takes it as a cue to proceed.

Amelia listens to the caller. Her pupils dilate and her mouth softens. For a moment, she appears to be thinking, then she says, "Yes, I'd love to. Can I bring Marcus?" She winks at me. "Yes, that would be fine."

Amelia tells me over dessert that we have a jogging date tomorrow morning. We decide to skip a TV movie and go to bed. Amelia slips into a long cotton nightgown and brushes her teeth. I stroll out into the yard and pee before trotting back into her bedroom. Amelia folds back the covers and pats a space beside her pillow. I jump up and snuggle beside her. "God, it's been a long time since I've been this happy," she says, tucking me next to her chin. She smells of spearmint mouthwash and Noxzema. I lick her smooth cheek and she scratches my back. I listen to the ticking clock on the night stand and slowly drift to sleep.

Special

Roz parked in the bus-loading zone. She slung her purse over her left shoulder and headed upstairs toward the principal's office.

A secretary was typing behind a computer monitor. She was a grandmotherly woman with a cloud of gray curls and soft amber eyes. She smiled weakly when Roz approached.

"Where's my son, Toby?" Roz asked, organized and efficient.

"Behind the door to the right," the secretary said, still typing.

Roz frowned and straightened her skirt. She had wanted to be an independent career woman when she was young. But the boredom of work plunged her deep into despair. Thinking she could repair her self-esteem, she married her best friend of eight years—a patient man who listened with his heart as well as his ears. A year later they had a son who developed slower than other children. The strain of raising a disabled child drove Roz to distraction. She fell in love with a co-worker who drove a Jaguar and who never left home without a wallet full of hundreds. His dark curls and perfectly clipped mustache reminded her of Tom Selleck in his better days and she abandoned the family she thought she had wanted.

Three years later, after her yearlong divorce and custody battles, she and her lover broke up. He wasn't getting enough attention because of her son, a boy who drifted from one activity to the next and who never followed directions.

"He's autistic," Roz explained.

"He's crazy," said her lover.

Roz knocked on the principal's door and was immediately told to come in. Toby, a tall, lanky ten-year old, slumped in a chair. He stared up at his mother with vacant brown eyes. "Head," Toby said, patting the top of his shaggy curls. It was the first word of a song Toby sang with his speech therapist. But unlike other children, he sang it indiscriminately, annoying everyone around him.

Roz shook Ms. Woo's hand and seated herself next to Toby. She folded her hands in her lap and listened. Ms. Woo explained that Toby had stared off into space for nearly forty minutes, then refused to go outside when the bell rang for recess. His teacher had tried to distract Toby into paying attention, but Toby couldn't be broken from his trance.

"… shoulders, knees and toes, knees and toes," Toby sang.

"It may have been a mild epileptic seizure," Roz said, trying to ignore her son's antics.

Ms. Woo nodded, as if she was familiar with the specifics. "I'm afraid we'll have to send him back into special ed," Ms. Woo said. "That's where they have the staff to help him with this disorder."

"I understand," Roz said, although in her heart she didn't.

At home, Toby was the model of a perfectly incapable son. Once, during a visit with an out-of-town guest, he ran into the street. In the middle of dinner, he would throw himself on the floor and scream and cry for no apparent reason. He would lie still on his back in the tub with the water all around his body and refuse to move even after the water was drained. Other times, he would stare off into space, incoherent, oblivious to everything around him. Roz's lover had said it was too high a price to pay for Roz's affection.

Grabbing Toby's hand and leading him down the stairs to the car, Roz noticed a crowd. They stood around the playground, twenty of them, give or take, clumped around the sand box, women mostly, stay-at-home moms, their T-shirts and cotton shorts refreshingly cool under a hot sky slipping fast to gray that the day felt like the inside of a metal mixing bowl, steely and suffocating. Roz stood beside the car with her hand on the knob while Toby patted his shoulders and sang to himself. She watched the kids hang upside down from the monkey bars, their belly buttons showing. A deep frown creased her face. If only, she wondered, knowing the futility of the wish. Unlocking the door, she said, "Stop singing that song and get in." Miraculously, Toby obeyed. She bent down to buckle him into the seat. Their eyes met. He saw her.

"Go?" he asked.

She nodded, thinking of the other children, wishing her son could be normal, but loving him nevertheless.

Cut Above the Rest

After hearing from her Harvard friends only once and not having any luck finding a job as an entry-level economist one-year short of a degree, Becky decided to enroll at the Santa Rosa Beauty College and become a licensed cosmetologist. With her long brown hair pulled into a simple bun and her face without make-up, Becky emerged as someone quaintly mature in a crowd of aspiring hairstylists with cherry bomb red hair and powdered white faces dressed in gray smocks and black leather shoes.

Some of the students Becky recognized from high school. Rodriguez, a slim young man with black hair slicked straight down his back and a goatee on his narrow chin, teased her. "Our Lady of the Perpetual Frown," he said, narrowing his slanted eyes and laughing. Tina, whom Becky remembered as a high school drop out with a drop-dead figure, even after giving birth to twins at seventeen, squealed in unison with Melody, the class clown, who called Becky, "The Harvard Could-Of-Been Graduate." Assaulted by cruel jokes and mean laughter, Becky focused on washing her mannequin's head with fierce concentration, often yanking the synthetic auburn hair until it snapped from its plastic skull.

Later, after six hours of cutting, dying, perming and styling, Becky went across the street to Triumph's Pub for an Irish cream coffee. Her favorite part of the day was sitting beside the iron black wood burning stove and watching the sun set through the picture window and the fairy lights of downtown ignite like fireflies. Becky had moved out of her parents' home in August after months of sullen silence. Her father, who had disappointed her before, tried to apologize with sweet, encouraging words. "Einstein said imagination was more important than knowledge," he'd tell her.

"You should have imagined $12,000," Becky would snap. "Then I wouldn't be wasting my life with a bunch of goons and styling gel." Becky's father would stare at the broken lip of his wing-tipped shoes. "I'm sorry," he'd say. Becky had heard the words before, when her father had stolen a Barbie doll for her birthday and had been arrested for shoplifting. Even though the charges had been dropped, Becky never forgave him. "You can't control yourself," she'd say.

By September, when her Harvard friends were buying books for classes, Becky started a part-time job at Johnny's Pool Hall as a coat check girl to pay the $300 rent for a room in her former high school math teacher's home. In her pocket she kept a love note from Chase, a girl Becky had met at a sorority party, written three months before Becky's

Harvard career ended. "I love the way you look when you study," Chase wrote. "It makes my palms sweat like I'm working out." Although Becky had her mail forwarded, she never received another letter from Chase. She tried hard not to think of the bulky football girl who had tackled her heart and won. Becky also tried not to think of her father. The one time she dropped by to visit she found him slumped over a set of cards at the dining room table, shuffling and reshuffling, contemplating how much he was going to bet in a game against himself.

Since then, on nights when she wasn't working, she lounged at Triumph's Pub and watched the night deepen into a relaxing atmosphere of couples playing darts, drinking their third Guinness, laughing, with their arms linked around each other's backs. When the couples left toward midnight, Becky would order a heavy rum drink she called a zombie and let her mind dissolve into foam. Dizzy with grief and unexpressed longing, she would kiss the stuffed head of a smiling moose before falling asleep on the black leather couch until Zero, the bartender, woke her up at two a.m. when he closed.

"Need a ride tonight?" Zero would ask.

"No, I'll call home," she'd say.

In the dark amber hall, with its dense wood-paneled walls and mirrored plaques emblazoned with the names of imported beers, Becky would drop a quarter and a dime into the pay phone and dial Bob Stone's number.

On her second day back from Harvard, Becky had waltzed across the campus of her old high school and had stepped into Mr. Stone's third period calculus class and cried. Disconcerted, Mr. Stone took her aside and drew a horizontal line with arrows in both directions. He placed a dot above the line and said, "Sorrow knows no infinity." When that didn't comfort her, he said he would think of something that would.

Weeks later, after dinner with Mr. Stone and his wife at their cozy restored Victorian, he invited Becky to move into the room behind the garage which he had used as an office once, then later converted into a bedroom for his teenage daughter, Sarah, who was attending U.C. Berkeley on a volley ball scholarship. Unaware of any complications, Becky unloaded her trunks and filled the dressers with her T-shirts and jeans, believing in the peacefulness of new beginnings. Only Lucy, who missed the routine of motherhood, would nag Becky about little things: eating the last piece of bread, misplacing the measuring cup for the laundry detergent, reading Shakespeare out loud. After a while, Becky tired of the accusations. She spent very little time with the Stones, perhaps one evening a month in front of the big screen TV with a movie she had rented and microwave popcorn she had bought at Food 4 Less.

When Becky called for a ride home, it was Lucy who often answered in her sultry after hour's voice. Since Sarah had left for college, Lucy took sedatives and mood-regulators for a peculiar disorder that flowed through her body in tiny ripples, causing her to overreact to anything that might break her fragile routine. Becky, who was too drunk for a fight, would hang up the phone.

"I'll drive you," Zero said. Becky shook her head, refusing his kindness. In the winter, Zero would stand under the awning with Becky holding an umbrella over her shiny brown hair until she was safe in the cab. Neither one spoke. Sometimes, while they were waiting, Zero would drape his coat over Becky's shoulders and press her close until she stopped shaking. In spite of a dark bulk that intimidated strangers, there was a tenderness about him that radiated like the warmth from his hands.

Alone, Becky would stagger up Orchard Street and crawl into her rented room and lay on the small bed while clutching a pillow to muffle her inconsolable sobs. Sometimes she'd write a sloppy love letter to Chase, accusing her of arrogant selfishness, or if the mood struck, she'd compose a hate letter to her father, reprimanding him for years of whimsical, unthinking passion that led him to gamble and lose her respect and love. In the morning, she'd tear up the letters as if they were nothing but junk mail. She'd shower and dress. On her way through the house, she'd stop in the master bedroom and slip a couple of Lucy's prescription pills from the nightstand into her pocket before joining the Stones for an intimate breakfast of bananas and English muffins, orange juice and coffee.

Later, she'd take the city transit downtown to the beauty college for another day of working on elderly models who chitchatted about the fascinating adventures of their soap opera lives. There was Julia, a grandmother of four, who came in weekly to have her nails painted a pearly rose. "I've loved many men, but none as much as Richard," she'd say. He was the 30-year-old carpenter she met when her daughter hired him to replace a rotten board around the living room window. Julia had admired the rippled muscles in his back and had asked him if he would look at a creaking floorboard in her bedroom. He agreed.

Three days later, he moved in. Permanently. They'd be married next June on a beach in Maui. Julia now worked out at Nautilus and was thinking about joining a tanning salon to prepare for the event.

There was Xia, a tiny Asian woman with thinning hair, who snapped her fingers and cursed in Mandarin whenever Becky did something wrong. "Too much bangs," Xia said. "I want to look white like Marilyn Monroe." And although the platinum blond dye worked, the effect left Xia cursing for a refund. Becky's instructor and supervisor, Ms. Wong, comforted Xia with a coupon for free beauty supplies at Regis and a promise to have one of her top students, Rodriguez, fix up the botched hairstyle.

Then there was Mrs. Fulkerson, a retired airline stewardess and widow, who flipped through back issues of *People* and *Vogue* pointing to the celebrities, saying, "Make me look like this. Make me look like that," always imagining a new beginning that would somehow end better. When Becky raised her shears, Mrs. Fulkerson would cover her eyes. "Oh, please, don't do it," she screamed, loud enough for the other students to glance at Becky's station. "I just want a quarter of an inch off the ends. Nothing drastic, do you hear?"

At the end of ten months and fifty-two bad haircuts, perms, and dye jobs, Becky felt she could not satisfy any of her clients. Not even Victoria who blamed her stunning burgundy hair and coy curls for getting her involved with a twenty-five year old scam artist. "He wouldn't have taken advantage of me if I looked like his mother," she sobbed. Immediately after Victoria left with a blunt bob from Tina, Becky quit the beauty college and headed across the street for a zombie. She fingered the vial of pills she had collected from Lucy's bedroom over the last six months—some black as the dye she used on Mrs. Leete's hair, some as white as the half moons that appeared when she pushed Mrs. Young's cuticles back. A few of the regulars greeted Becky when she stepped through the oak door with its stained glass window, but Becky didn't return the gesture. She didn't want to talk, because that meant listening, something she did all day.

At the counter, Zero polished a shot glass and flashed his ivory smile. "You're early." Becky nodded and set a ten beside the register.

"One Irish cream," Zero said.

"No, a zombie."

Zero arched his squiggly eyebrows but didn't say a word. Becky slumped on the black leather couch where she had fallen asleep three dozen times before and counted the pills in her lap. Thirty-six. She wondered briefly what they would do to her body, if they would sufficiently clog her mind and open her veins. She dumped the pills back into their plastic container and waited for her drink. In the flickering firelight, she examined her short, stubby, colorless nails. Her whole life seemed colorless. Back in high school, she had been hopeful: for an Ivy League education far from home, for developing long lasting friendships with Harvard graduates with futures as bright as her own. She had no intention of spending her days with girls who looked forward to rock concerts or meeting young men who cared more about fashion than about the New York Times best seller list. Becky rubbed her palms against her forehead and sighed.

The whole idea of devoting her youth, her talents, her future to clipping and primping women who laughed and loved and hated with more passion and purpose than herself made her weak and nauseous. And, alone.

A few moments later, Zero sat down beside her without the drink she had ordered. Becky frowned and moved closer to the fire. Zero clasped his hands between his knees and leaned forward as if he was listening. "When I was seventeen," he said, "I wanted to be a wrestler, but I broke my sternum and punctured a lung during a match and almost died. It took me years to recover my self-esteem, not to mention my will to live and my fabulous figure." He laughed, patting his belly. "Well, as you can see, I'm still working on my figure."

Becky leaned back against the couch. "Why are you telling me this?"

"Because Rodriguez was in last night and he told me you had not registered for the state exam. I'm worried you'll quit."

"I already have. Today."

Zero nodded. "Then I guess I'm too late." For a long moment, he stared at the fire. Shadows of crackling crimson flames flickered across his soft black eyes, broad flat nose and solemnly puckered thick lips. Becky thought Zero looked as painfully sad as her father had the night he confessed to her how he had miscalculated his bets and lost $60,000 on roulette.

"I'm sorry," her father said. There were tears in his voice. Becky had never told anyone the real reason why she hadn't finished Harvard. Her shame resurfaced in dreams where her father tiptoed downstairs when everyone was asleep and started the Dodge Caravan and drove to Tahoe with the cash inside his wool coat. Each time she woke up gasping for air, shouting, "Don't do it, Daddy," and each time she cried herself back to sleep.

It was five-thirty and the after work crowd clattered into the barroom for beers and darts and long-winded conversations. Zero slapped his thighs. "Gotta get back to work." Becky unscrewed the bottle, dumped the pills into her palm, and held out her hand. Zero stared at them, then at her.

"Are you sure?" he asked. Becky nodded, taking his hand and folding his dark fingers over the thirty-six black and white pills.

"You're a brave woman," Zero said, pocketing the pills. He offered Becky his hand.

"Would you like to go dancing with me after I close up? There's a cute little jazz club down the street that plays till four. I could teach you how to dance."

Becky shook her head. "I don't think so."

"Why not?"

"I loved a woman once and she broke my heart."

"Women are always breaking my heart. But what's a guy supposed to do? Give up? Why, who's that poet who said it's better to have loved and lost than to have never loved at all?"

"Tennyson." Becky smiled. "Lord Alfred Tennyson."

Zero laughed and tossed the pills in the trash behind the counter. "That guy's smarter than Shakespeare. No suicides in his book."

Becky took a seat at the bar and fingered a cocktail napkin. "It's easier to give up than to move on."

"Hear, hear, I agree." Zero poured a coffee and slid it toward Becky. "No zombies for you." Becky stared at the steaming mug. The black coffee was as warm and comforting as Zero's eyes.

"I guess it wouldn't hurt to learn how to dance."

Zero winked. "Women always love a great dancer."

Hope in the Laundry Room

The first thing Josh noticed about the young woman was her black gabardine suit. It hung loose and limp from her shoulders as if she had lost a lot of weight, but couldn't afford to buy a new suit.

Since working at The Laundry Room, Josh noticed how clothes defined people. Men with torn T-shirts, board shorts and flip flops, who tossed all their clothes into one washer and played the arcade games while their clothes dried, told classic stories of bachelorhood. The no-nonsense Old Navy favorites worn by students with backpacks slumped in front of the big screen TV pretending to study broadcasted listlessness. Mothers with their sweat pants and hair pulled back with scrunchies screamed haggard housewives. Boys with holes in their faded jeans told stories of backyard adventures. Girls with dresses so faded the tiny rosebuds looked like they had barely survived a rain storm whispered secrets of poverty and dreams of riches. Old men in impeccable black slacks and elderly women in paisley dresses, who shuffled in with their single baskets for the wash and fold service, hinted at old-fashioned pride. These were the people who populated The Laundry Room. Not thirty-something women dressed in black gabardine suits, no matter how big and ungainly those suits might be.

But Josh didn't ask the young woman the story behind her black gabardine suit. He just watched her from where he sat on a stool behind the register, stitching the inseam of a customer's slacks which still needed to be washed and pressed before five-thirty when the garment had been promised ready for pickup.

The young woman kept an odd, though regular, schedule. On Mondays, she would stop by at ten-thirty and load three washers. At noon, she would return and toss the loads into dryers. At two-thirty, she would stalk across the linoleum floors in her scuffed black heels and gather the clean clothes into plastic baskets and shove them into the trunk of her white Toyota Camry before speeding away.

After the young woman had been a patron of The Laundry Room for a few weeks, Josh told his roommates about her.

They were sitting in the living room watching the 49ers post-game commentary. The lights had been turned down low to save energy, which was Amir's idea, and the volume of the TV had been turned down even lower so they could talk, which was Mike's idea. Josh sat between them with his feet propped up on the coffee table which was littered with take-out boxes and beer cans on Mike's side, and neat stacks of *Forbes* and

Business Week on Amir's side.

"Is she stacked?" Mike asked, biting into a piece of leftover pizza. He chewed with his mouth open, wiping the grease around his lips with the back of his hand. Mike had a girlfriend who sometimes paid his rent when he didn't have enough money to cover his bills between his band's gigs, but a steady woman didn't stop him from ogling other women. Or touching them, for that matter. Or even taking them to bed.

Josh thought about the question, but not too long. He didn't want to seem obsessed by her, although he knew he was. "Not that I know. It's hard to tell because her clothes are so big on her."

Amir clucked his tongue on the roof of his mouth. "You don't want to be going after women who can't afford a proper wardrobe," he said. "If she can't afford decent clothes, not to mention her own washer and dryer, then she is not a good investment." Amir was a postgraduate business student with an undergraduate degree in public relations. He was planning on becoming a stock broker once he graduated with his MBA next year. "You should come with me next weekend to my sister's wedding. There will be lots of single women there. Her friends all come from wealthy families. Dating one of them would be a good investment."

Mike scoffed. "Not if he just wants to bang the chick, man. Why do you have to always turn everything into dollars and cents?"

"Good relationships are like good business partnerships. They return your investment to you. Find a woman who can take care of herself, and she'll be able to take care of you if something bad happens. If the woman is a financially spoiled brat with no common sense, or a working woman with no cash left after the bills are paid, you're wasting your time with her. The first woman will bleed you dry with her spending sprees. The second woman will not be able to contribute to your nest egg. I'm telling you, no woman is better than a bad woman, and a bad woman is any woman who will not return her investment tenfold. Understand?"

Mike swallowed the last bite of pizza and shook his head. "Don't listen to him, Josh. He's just a cynical old man who can't get laid."

Amir pursed his lips and sat up straight on the sofa. "That's not true. I'm waiting for the right woman. I don't want to ruin my chances of a good investment by squandering my seed with useless women who may, or may not, be lying about their birth control methods in an attempt to land a golden egg."

Mike leaned back into the sofa and rolled his eyes. "Whatever, man."

Josh picked up the empty pizza box and walked into the kitchen to throw it into the trash.

Amir followed him. "Will you come to the wedding with me?"

Josh thought about it. "What day again?"

"Next Sunday at three-thirty. The dinner starts at five. We should be home no later than nine in case you have to get up early." Amir leaned against the counter and crossed his arms over his button-down shirt. Amir always dressed impeccably, as though at any moment someone might show up to give him an interview. "I'm thinking of one woman in particular who would be great for you. Sarah. She's my sister's best friend. She just returned from Japan teaching English. She was able to pay off her student loans and she just got a job in the private sector. I'm not sure what she does, but I hear she gets paid well." For a long moment, Amir seemed to be thinking. "Oh, and yes, she's very pretty. She has long dark hair, strong bones, and 20/20 vision. You two would make attractive children."

Josh wondered how Amir pitched him to other women. He imagined Amir saying, "He's finishing up his bachelor's degree in child psychology. Yes, he loves children. Oh, and he's good-looking. Light brown hair and hazel eyes, small boned, but muscular. No, he's not funny. But he's a good listener. And he knows how to cook and sew. A real post-modern man. You have to meet him sometime."

If only Amir's assessments of people allowed for all the vagaries of common interests and chemistry, then Josh might have agreed to attend the wedding. But Amir didn't care whether a couple enjoyed hiking in the mountains together or found their bodies irresistible, he only cared about whether or not the partnership offered a positive cash-flow.

"I'm sorry," Josh said, unloading the dishwasher. "I have dinner with my parents that night and I can't disappoint them. I haven't seen them in months, and I can't afford to piss them off. I still rely on them to help with tuition. Maybe next time."

Amir clucked his tongue. "You're right, you'll be sorry. This time next year Sarah will be engaged, to another man. Just you wait and see."

A few minutes after Amir left, Mike entered to grab another beer from the fridge. He cracked it open, slurping up the foam, and smacked his lips loudly. "You ought to hang out at my next gig," he said. "Tons of chicks throw their bras onstage when we sing, 'Crawl Out of Nowhere.' The guys and I have more than enough ass to go around. How about it?"

Josh stacked the plates in the cupboard and thoughtfully shut the door. "I don't know," he said. He had been to one of Mike's gigs in a dimly lit bar shortly after he had moved into the apartment two years ago. All he remembered from that night was downing too many shots, having too many breasts flashed in his face, and waking up with the worse hangover he ever had. He didn't even remember whether or not he came home alone, and if he had entertained a woman, he wouldn't recognize her in a police lineup. "I have to get up early to work," he said.

"Man, you should quit that laundry place and get a job waiting tables. Chicks love waiters. I used to take one home a week instead of a tip." Mike gulped the remaining beer and crushed the can in his hand and tossed it into the sink.

"The recycling bin is right next to you," Josh said, staring at the crushed can on top of the plates and bowls in the sink.

"Yeah, whatever, man." Mike burped and walked away.

Josh sighed. He dumped the can in the recycling bin and ran hot water in the sink, scrubbing off the bits of dried cereal on the bowls before loading them into the dishwasher. He thought of the young woman in the too big suit leaning over the sink in her apartment, loading the dishes with the same efficient precision she used to sort and wash her clothes. He wondered if she had an IRA, or if her breasts were soft and real. But mostly, he just thought of her, breezing into and out of The Laundry Room with baskets full of clothes, her hips swaying underneath her baggy slacks, her worn heels clicking against the linoleum like a soundtrack, filling his work day with music and his night life with dreams.

***

On Monday, Josh watched the young woman in the black gabardine suit nudge the door of The Laundry Room open with her hip, her arms full with a basket of clothes. Josh wanted to excuse himself and help her, but his boss, Mr. Yokohama, an elderly man who spoke broken English and who was a tyrant for focus, was counting out the till from last night and giving him instructions for the week.

The young woman in the black gabardine suit selected the middle section of washers and sorted the clothes, left, center, right, with her usual determined precision, checking the clock on the wall over the bank of dryers to make sure she didn't spend too much time.

"I going to be out of town for two weeks," Mr. Yokohama said, zipping up the bank pouch. "I hoping you stop by and see night shift close okay."

"No problem," Josh said, glancing up just in time to see the young woman in the black gabardine suit slip out the door.

"I pay you extra for your time," Mr. Yokohama said. "You good man, you do good job, you like a son to me."

Josh nodded his thanks and felt the flush of embarrassment travel to his face. He was unaccustomed to praise from teachers, from bosses, from strangers, and the compliment left him feeling uneasy. He was responsible by nature. Even as a child, he picked up his room without being asked. Between customers, he would wipe down the machines, hem pants, stitch buttons back on blouses, and even polish the register. Of course, he would stop by The Laundry Room at ten to make sure the floor had been mopped and the cash register balanced even though he would be up at six to return to the place once again.

After Mr. Yokohama left, another rush of customers arrived with their baskets of laundry and torn items to be repaired. Josh was ringing up a customer during the busy lunch hour when the young woman in the black gabardine suit returned, unloading the wash and placing them into dryers. A silver glint flashed from her wrist, and Josh wondered if she had purchased a watch. By the time he had finished counting out the change for the customer, the young woman in the black gabardine suit had left. Josh slumped behind the counter, his heart deflated like all the air had been squeezed out of his chest.

In the early afternoon lull, Josh wiped down the washers, paying extra attention to the three washers the young woman in the black gabardine suit had used. At the bottom of the third washer, something clicked against the sides. He reached in and plucked out a tiny sterling silver charm with a broken clasp. The letters on the charm spelled HOPE. Josh curled his fingers around the cool letters, feeling his heart swell with a reason to speak with the young woman in the black gabardine suit.

But when she returned to pick up her clothes, Josh was busy with a customer on the phone who was asking for a price list of The Laundry Room's services. He put the caller on hold only to have Mr. Yokohama call in on the other line, alerting him that Stephanie, who was scheduled to work the three to ten shift, had come down with the flu. "You call other employees to see who can work for her, okay?" Josh swallowed, feeling his throat constrict, as the young woman in the black gabardine suit shoved her clothes into the last basket. The silver bracelet on her right wrist caught the afternoon rays as she pushed the door open with her hip and stepped into the parking lot.

***

Every day, for the rest of the week, Josh carried the silver HOPE charm in the front right pocket of his jeans. Between customers, he would reach into his pocket and caress the four-letters with the pad of his thumb. Sometimes, late at night when he couldn't sleep, he would trace the block letters with his index finger. He would curl his fist around the word and tuck his hand underneath his pillow and fall into a dreamless sleep.

Josh wondered what he would say to the young woman in the black gabardine suit on Monday when she returned with her three baskets full of clothes. He had scheduled an extra person to share his shift so he could delegate any tasks that might keep him from speaking with the young woman.

One night, Josh stood in front of the stove caressing the HOPE charm in the palm of his hand. He daydreamed about his future encounter with the young woman and how she would lift her face to the sound of his voice, how her lips would curl into a smile once he held out to her the HOPE charm she had been missing all week.

***

Steam rumbled from beneath the lid of the green beans. The pot of rice boiled over. Josh shoved the charm into his pocket, turned down the heat, and checked on the chicken in the oven. A crisp, burnt smell filled the room, and Josh flicked the switch on the hood, hoping the acrid smoke would leave before his roommates came home.

But Amir poked at the hard grains of rice on his plate and said, "Something's wrong. You never burn the rice."

Mike slurped from his can of beer and burped. "He's in love, stupid."

"In love?" Amir narrowed his gaze and studied Josh as if he was a foreign currency. "How did this happen?"

Josh ignored the question. "Maybe if you two pitched in once in a while instead of expecting me to do everything, the dinner would be perfect all the time."

Amir clucked his tongue on the roof of his mouth. "You always cook dinner. And you've never complained about it until now. What's changed?"

Mike chortled. "I told you, man, he's in love. See the goo-goo eyes?"

Amir squinted. "Who is she?"

When Josh didn't answer, Mike said, "It's that girl from the laundromat."

Amir shook his fork at Josh. "There's still time to come to my sister's wedding. I've already told Sarah about you."

"I'm going to my parents' house."

"Cancel," Amir said. "Your future depends on it."

Mike laughed. "He's not looking to get married, man. He's looking to get laid."

Josh's fork clattered against his plate. "Both of you, stop it!" Josh glowered at Mike who continued laughing and Amir who raised his eyebrows in mock innocence. Without waiting for either one to reply, Josh scooted his chair back and carried his plate of half-eaten chicken, rice, and green beans to the sink.

Alone in his room, with the door closed, Josh flopped onto his mattress. He reached into his pocket and removed the HOPE charm. The last rays of the setting sun glinted off the letters, creating the impression of shooting stars.

Neither of his roommates understood him. He wasn't looking to get married. He wasn't looking to get laid. He didn't even know if he was looking.

All he knew was he had found something precious and valuable and rare. Something beyond a good-looking woman in an oversized suit. Something beyond the four letters he held in his hand. What he had found was that magnetic pull to unravel the mystery of another human being. The object he held in his hand was the key that might unite them, if only for a moment.

That Sunday, at his parents' house for dinner, Josh's mother asked him gently, "Are you seeing anyone?"

She sat beside him in the dress she had worn to church. Her hand absently twirled the necklace of pearls at her throat. She smelled of gardenias and homemade bread. It was comforting to sit beside her, a refuge as sweet and safe as the shady branches of a secluded tree.

Josh thought about the young woman in the black gabardine suit. He wasn't seeing her. He wasn't even speaking with her. Yet.

He shrugged. "Not really."

His father, a tall man who always sat up straight and placed his fork down and swallowed before speaking, said, "He's focused on his studies, Miriam. He has no time to date."

His mother seemed to understand there was something more, something Josh was not telling anyone.

Later, while helping his mother rinse dishes and load them into the dishwasher, Josh said, "I found a silver charm that I think belongs to a woman. I'm going to see her on Monday, but I don't know what to say."

His mother stopped rinsing a plate. The water ran over her hand, pooling at the bottom of the sink. Her bright green eyes cut through him as though she were seeing not into the past or the future, but here and now. "Just say whatever comes to mind," she advised. "Don't plan it or force it. Just speak."

Josh swallowed. He rearranged the silverware. "I've wanted to talk to her for weeks, but there's never a chance."

His mother turned off the water, dried her hands, and pulled Josh into her arms for a hug. "There's never a good time. There is only the time you have right now. Don't waste it."

Josh nodded, feeling tears well up in his eyes and not knowing why. The silver HOPE charm rested against his thigh, burning with an uncanny warmth.

Tomorrow he would speak with the young woman in the black gabardine suit. He would say whatever was on his mind. No matter what. He would do it.

***

Josh made sure Stephanie was at the register when the young mystery woman arrived. He stood in front of the full length mirror in the seamstress room in the back and smoothed his hands over his blue button-down shirt before shoving them into the front pockets of his jeans. The silver HOPE charm warmed between his sweaty fingers. He glanced at the clock and stepped back into The Laundry Room just as she pulled her white Toyota Camry into a parking slot.

Josh's heart hammered in his chest as he held the door open for her. The woman glanced over her basket of laundry and smiled at him. She had soft brown eyes and coffee-stained teeth. "Thanks," she said.

"May I help you with the other baskets?" he asked.

Her eyebrows slanted together. "How do you know I have more?"

"You're a regular," Josh said. "I know all the regulars. Except you."

She said her name was Tracy. She was a paralegal for a real estate attorney downtown. "He's bills by the minute," she explained. "So I've learned to live by the minute." While she sorted clothes, Josh introduced himself as a student at the university who worked full-time at The Laundry Room while finishing his bachelor's in child psychology. "I'll graduate next year," he explained. He didn't want to tell her that he had nothing planned after that. He was embarrassed by his entire future being a blank slate.

Before she left, Josh held out the sterling silver HOPE charm. "I found this in one of the washers you used last week and wondered if it was yours."

She gasped. "My charm! You found it!"

He placed it in her palm.

"I thought I lost it," she said, her brown eyes misting. "How can I ever thank you?"

He glanced at the clock. "I'll think of something by the time you come back," he said.

She tilted her head to the side. Her brown hair curled into a question mark against the lapel of her oversized suit. She hustled out the doors, placed her stacked baskets in the trunk, and drove off.

Josh watched her leave, wondering why he felt the HOPE he had given back to her swell within his chest.

When Tracy returned, Josh was sitting behind the counter stitching a button back onto a shirt. Stephanie was on her ten minute break, so when the phone rang, he had to answer it.

Tracy emptied her washers into dryers. Before she left, she waved to Josh. He lifted up his hand as if to signal, *Just one minute*, but she must have been in a hurry because she didn't wait.

After hanging up the phone, Josh picked up the Yellow Pages and flipped through the section on attorneys. Maybe he would call each one until he found her. But he stopped himself before picking up the phone. Be patient, he thought. She'll be back at two-thirty.

The hours ticked by slowly. Each second seemed longer than the last. Finally, at two-thirty, Tracy pulled up into a parking slot and removed her baskets and sauntered into The Laundry Room.

"Hey, I've thought of something," Josh said, trying to sound casual, not desperate. "How about you go out with me on a date?"

The smile she once had for him disappeared. "I can't," she explained.

"Oh, I'm sorry, I didn't know you had a boyfriend," Josh stammered, feeling his face flush with his assumption that she was single.

"No, I'm a widow, actually. My husband died in the war with Iraq. It's my son I'm concerned about." She shoved the clothes into a basket as she explained she had a seven-year old son, Liam, named after his father, who needed constant care. Liam attended a special day class and came home from school at three. She designed her entire life around his schedule. That's why she came to The Laundry Room on Mondays, so she would not have to take Liam with her. "He tends to run away," she explained. "And I have no one to watch him."

Her parents lived in Oregon and her in-laws hadn't spoken to her since Liam had been diagnosed with developmental delay when he was three. The HOPE charm Josh had found had been a gift from her husband when they were dating. She had only recently started wearing it again. She had lost twenty-eight pounds from mourning and had no time to shop with Liam needing constant care.

"Then let me take you shopping instead," Josh suggested.

Tracy resisted, at first, but the longer Josh spoke with her about what he knew about children's development from the classes he had taken, the more she softened.

"I get off at three," he said. "But I can leave early since I've been working extra for my boss while he's away. Just let me tell Stephanie I'm leaving."

"You want to shop today?" she asked.

He nodded, recalling his mother's words. "I've wanted to get to know you for weeks and I've just found the courage to talk to you today. I may not have the courage to go shopping with you tomorrow or next week."

She absently caressed one of Liam's shirts. Considering his words, "Okay," she said. "You can follow me home."

Liam was a skinny boy with tumbleweed hair and a gap-toothed smile. He loped off the bus, dragging his back pack behind him like a blanket. Liam glanced at his mother, then at Josh. He dropped his back pack and wrapped his arms around Josh's legs. "Up," he said, like a toddler.

Tracy giggled. "He likes you."

Josh picked Liam up. He was much heavier than he looked. But he was warm and trusting and full of smiles. Josh felt his heart break open and love pour through him. "I like him, too."

They piled into Tracy's Camry, since Liam preferred things he knew. "Change terrifies him," Tracy explained.

"Where does he like to shop?" Josh asked.

"He likes the mall, but it's dangerous," Tracy said. "I lost him once and the security guards weren't helpful. Liam doesn't talk much. He can't say his address or phone number or even his last name. I was so scared. I had just lost my husband. I didn't want to lose my son, too." Her voice trembled with emotion. "Finally, I found him outside the cutlery store staring at the rotating Swiss army knife display. I was so relieved I didn't care that he threw a fit when I tried to take him home. We just stayed until the mall closed."

Josh tried to imagine the terror Tracy must have felt. No wonder she went to work and ran her errands on her breaks and spent the rest of her time inside her apartment with Liam where it was safe. "I'll stay with him at the cutlery store while you shop," Josh said.

"Are you sure?" she asked.

"I'm positive," Josh said. He had studied special needs children in one of his courses last semester. How hard could it be? "You need a new suit and we aren't leaving until you find one that fits."

Tracy's smile broadened. "You are a brave man," she said.

***

As soon as they pulled into the parking lot, Liam squealed with delight and kicked the back of Josh's seat. The force of the kicks reverberated against Josh's lower back, pushing him forward slightly.

Tracy parked and gave Josh her cell number. "Just in case something goes wrong," she said.

What could possibly go wrong? Josh wondered. Liam was small. Sure, he had a mean kick, but he walked funny.

"Ready?" Tracy opened the door to the backseat and called over her shoulder to Josh. "Get ready to grab him. He's fast."

Josh nodded. *How hard could this be?* Maybe the boy was difficult for Tracy who was apparently petite and slender, but Josh was tall and athletic. He lifted weights twice a week and ran two miles almost every day.

Liam bolted outside as soon as his seatbelt was released. His arms and legs flapped like sheets in the wind as he loped across the parking lot, not taking notice of moving vehicles. Josh instinctively ran after him, pumping his arms and swinging his legs in a hearty sprint. Tracy raced after them, shouting, "I warned you!" Josh eventually caught up with Liam, hooking his arm around the boy's waist and hoisting him away from a parked car that had shifted into reverse.

Tracy gasped. "You got him."

Josh pressed the squirming boy against his heart that was catapulting all over his chest. The flailing arms and legs yanked his hair and kicked his thighs, but Josh refused to let go. He strode across the parking lot with Tracy beside him.

"We can leave," Tracy said.

Josh huffed and puffed, carrying the tantruming boy in his arms. "We're not leaving," he said.

Tracy jogged ahead and held open the glass door. Once safely inside, Josh set Liam down. The boy splayed on the linoleum floor, biting his fingers until he suddenly looked up and noticed the neon red circle surrounding the rotating Swiss army knife display outside the cutlery store down the aisle. He sprung up and ran with single-minded purpose. Josh sprinted after him, weaving between shoppers laden with bags.

Tracy's heels clip-clopped behind him.

Once Liam reached the display, he stood still. His eyes grew wide, transfixed by the silver blades spinning around, opening and closing, like a steel acrobat. Josh slumped against the wall beside the display, breathing in and out, in and out, trying to steady his nerves.

Tracy caught up with them. "This was a bad idea."

Josh shook his head. "I need the exercise," he said, flashing a crooked smile at her. "See, he's fine."

Tracy gazed at her immobile son.

"Go shop. Have fun." Josh tried to reassure her. "I'll call you if I need you."

For a long moment, Tracy studied him. Josh wondered what she was thinking, but was too afraid to ask. Finally, she bent to kiss Liam on the top of the head and wave good-bye to Josh. "I'll be at Macy's at the other end of the mall," she said.

"We'll be right here," Josh said. "Unless he decides to ogle the display at Victoria's Secret. Then I'll call you." Josh winked.

A tentative smile formed on her face. "Thanks." She backed up slowly, then turned around, and strode away.

Josh watched her hips sway beneath her baggy slacks. He wished he could go with her and help her pick out a new suit. But he was here, outside the cutlery store, with Liam whose intent focus on the steel blades reminded him of his mother when she strode into The Laundry Room and sorted her clothes.

After a few minutes, Josh slid down the wall and sat next to Liam who stood with his hands plastered to the window. Liam's eyes tracked the revolving blades. Josh tried to remember when accurate tracking of the eyes developed in a child. Six months? Eight months? He wasn't sure. Searching in his pockets for something to engage Liam, Josh found a piece of gum, wallet, keys, and a stray quarter. He removed the quarter and dangled it in front of Liam's face, trying to break his concentration.

"Liam, look at this." Josh waited until Liam's gaze registered the object. Slowly, Josh moved the quarter toward the ground. Liam bent closer. Josh twirled the quarter on its side. Liam dropped to his knees and bowed his head to examine the spinning quarter. Josh noted Liam's intent focus matched the same intensity he had devoted to the revolving Swiss army knife display. But as soon as the quarter fell onto its side, Liam bounced back up and plastered his hands against the glass, his gaze once more transfixed by the twirling silver blades.

Josh pocketed the quarter and leaned his head against the wall, observing Liam. In the three years Josh had studied child development, he had never spent any time with real children. All of Josh's learning had been gleaned from textbooks and lectures from doctors and specialists who professed their expertise through PowerPoint presentations or university published books. No one had ever presented Josh with an actual case study.

Liam was the first child Josh had witnessed who didn't fall into the normal spectrum. Looking at Liam's clothes—a brown and beige striped polo shirt and black pants with an elastic waistband to fit over Liam's Ethiopian-like belly—Josh might have imagined Liam was a typical seven-year-old boy who collected Matchbox cars and played basketball in the driveway. But as soon as Liam spoke his halting, monosyllabic words, anyone would know Liam was different.

Josh rubbed his calves, remembering how hard he had to sprint in the parking lot to catch up with Liam. Liam's floppy rag doll muscles lacked coordination but not speed and Liam's attention span rivaled any adult. Josh didn't know if Liam could read or write or even count to ten. But Josh did know Liam was fascinated by bright, shining objects that caught the light as they moved.

Liam continued to stand in front of the revolving Swiss army knife display, captivated by its rhythmic movement. Josh continued to sit on the linoleum beside him, fascinated by the enigmatic boy he wanted desperately to understand.

***

A half hour later, Tracy returned, holding a dress bag over the crook of one arm and a small shopping bag in the other. At first, Josh didn't recognize her. He had always paid more attention to her clothes than her face. She was no longer wearing the black gabardine suit. Instead, she was dressed in a buttery-colored suit that showcased her gorgeous curves. Her dark hair, brown eyes and tawny skin provided a great contrast to the suit. She looked like the "after" photos shown in diet pill ads. There was also a difference in her gait, less hurried and more relaxed, that seemed to add a bounce to each step. Or maybe, Josh thought, it was the new set of caramel-colored heels she sported.

She twirled around once before him. "What do you think?" she asked.

Josh smiled. "Well, if I was my roommate, Mike, I'd say you look hot. But, if I was my roommate, Amir, I'd say you look like a million dollars."

"But you're not Mike or Amir," Tracy said. "You're you. What do *you* think?"

Josh didn't want to say she looked more poised and polished than he could ever imagine being. "I bet you can't wash that at The Laundry Room," he said. "I bet it's dry clean only."

She shook her head in mock frustration. "Most women complain men can't make a commitment. I just want a compliment."

Josh laughed. "Okay, already. You look beautiful. The suit really fits you."

She smiled. "How have you and Liam been?"

Josh turned toward the boy. "We've been doing well, haven't we, Liam?"

Liam didn't even blink.

Tracy pursed her lips and anxiously twisted the bag in her hand. "How are we going to get him out of here? The last time we were here he threw a fit when I tried to leave."

Josh thought for a long time. Nothing in his studies helped him find a solution, but something in his recent experience sparked a possibility. "Wait here," he said. "I have an idea." Josh strolled into the cutlery store and signaled for the clerk. "Do you mind turning off the display?" he asked. "My kid won't leave as long as it's spinning."

The clerk glanced outside at Tracy and Liam. "No problem," he said, bending down to flick a switch.

Josh strode outside. He removed the quarter in his pocket and tossed it back and forth between his two hands. "Okay, Liam, let's go."

Liam stared at the dark display, then at the quarter bouncing back and forth between Josh's hands. Slowly, Josh stepped back toward the glass doors. Liam tentatively followed him. A minute later, they were outside in the bright afternoon sunlight. Josh pocketed the quarter.

Liam whimpered.

"He wants you to do it again," Tracy said.

Josh felt like a magician. He pulled out the quarter and tossed it back and forth between his hands. Sunlight winked off George Washington's profile. Liam stared. Tracy grabbed Liam's hand and nudged him forward. Josh glanced around for moving vehicles as he walked toward

Tracy's Camry, careful to keep the quarter moving back and forth between his hands.

Later that night, after closing up The Laundry Room, Josh returned to his apartment. He scrunched on the couch between Mike and Amir who were watching *The Tonight Show*. Josh didn't wait until the commercial break to tell them about his day.

Mike sat up and crumpled the empty bag of potato chips in his hands. "Did she buy new underwear, too?" he asked.

Josh shrugged. "I don't know."

"Well, why don't you? Didn't you get some?" he asked.

Amir clucked his tongue. "It's best he didn't touch her. A handicapped child is a liability, not an asset." Amir picked up a magazine and flipped through its pages. He pointed to a glossy photo of a disabled child next to a graph. "See here? It costs $6,000 a month to take care of one of these kids. You don't even make that much. How are you going to support this woman and her kid? My advice is to never speak with her again. You'll only regret it later when your bank account is dry."

Mike snorted. "But she's hot! Can't he just bang her once in The Laundry Room during her lunch break?"

Amir shook his head. "And what if she becomes pregnant from that one mishap? He'll be stuck for life!"

Josh stood up. "I'm going to bed." No one bothered to say goodnight to him.

Alone, in his room, Josh buried his head into his pillow and wept. He wished he had never confided in his roommates. They didn't understand him. Josh wasn't interested in banging Tracy or financially supporting Liam. He just wanted to spend time with them like he spent time with his parents. He wanted to know the two of them for who they were, not how their clothes defined them. He rolled onto his back and recalled how he told the clerk to turn off the display. He remembered tossing the quarter back and forth between his hands. Liam followed the bouncing quarter as though he were in a trance. Josh sniffed back his tears and smiled. He was proud he was able to guide the boy safely out of the mall and back to his mother's car without a tantrum, something no one had ever done before, something only he could do, and that was what he wanted, to do that over and over again, for as long as Tracy and Liam would let him.

Heatwave

Peter had started meditating, once in the morning and once at night. I asked him if it made a difference.

"No, I still hear voices telling me to do things I don't want to think about. It gets me more nervous, sitting there and listening, not knowing what else I can do, except act." He leaned back against the cushions of the couch, crossed his arms behind his neck and closed his eyes.

"What do the voices tell you to do?"

"Kiss you."

"You've always wanted to kiss me. What's different?" I demanded. He ignored me.

"Am I attractive?" Peter asked. He was, tall and lean and athletic, with more muscle tone than a gym teacher.

"No, you're fat and ugly. Absolutely hideous. It's no wonder you're afraid to kiss me. You might turn into a toad."

"Shut up," Peter said.

I shut up.

When the first sunlight broke through gray clouds and sparkled against dewy grass and rain-drenched trees, a crisp smell grew over the city, washing away winter's loneliness. Gradually, the warmth burned through and ignited wildfires over the county. Patches of dry grass burst into yellow flames. Black plumes billowed across the golden fields. Cars stopped along the highway; people stared eagerly at summer's destruction. Sunlight had struck one weed that exploded into devil's flames. Tongues of fire danced a jig across the landscape and scarred the once beautiful earth.

I sat on the porch watching the gray whispers fade into blue sky as the fire department doused the flames from a wildfire off Highway 1. As I let my arms dangle by my side, a hot sputter of sunlight blazed against the blond hairs of my forearm. Inside, Peter stirred the iced tea and poured it into long tall glasses. The clink of ice against glass comforted me as much as the moist beaded coolness against my hot and tired skin. We sat side by side, not speaking. We watched the gray smoke trail into nothingness against the vast washed-out canvas that bordered our world.

Peter pulled out his harmonica and played "Angry Young Man." The notes rattled a loose pane in the window behind us. An ice cream truck rumbled down the street, hiccupping "Pop Goes the Weasel." Peter stopped in mid-tune, letting the dizzy laughter of children chase away the music in his throat. I placed my arm around his shoulder and lay my head against the curve of his neck. My cold wet fingers slipped under his T-shirt and traced a circle around his hard nipple. He quivered like a string plucked on a guitar. His heart beat quickened underneath my hand. I closed my eyes and listened. Thump-thump. Thump-thump.

Peter's lips grazed my forehead. I tilted my head back and opened my eyes and saw him staring at me in distant wonder.

"Kiss me, you fool."

Peter shook his head, fitting the harmonica in the space between his lips, letting the passion and the anger and the disappointment vibrate through the metal teeth, creating a tense and lightheaded song.

The wildfire continued throughout the night, and another ignited over the weekend, setting a record for the fifth consecutive year that I had been here. Although I had no TV, I could guess what the pictures were like. The same stock footage of heroic firemen hosed down hungry flames. Sometimes they rescued people. More likely, they fought alone. Man against nature, as my English professor used to say, is a classic story-line.

Peter cared little for the fire reports. He moped around the house on his days off as a dance choreographer at a local studio. Sometimes he dressed in my husband's clothes, the denim and khakis falling loose around his joints where they puffed up around my husband's thick waist and massive thighs. The T-shirts swallowed the graceful lines of his powerful chest and flat stomach. Only his arms, pitifully white, bulged into a map of many rivers, blue veins coursing under the translucent skin. They were beautiful arms, arms that held me gently when I cried, arms that could lift and bend and break loneliness into a thousand pieces, scattering them to the wind.

I stayed outside when Peter visited, preferring the scrutiny of curious neighbors to the dangerous heat inside. Peter either napped on the couch or read one of his many library books on geologic disturbances. Sometimes he sat outside with me and played his harmonica. I introduced him to the neighbors as a cousin from San Diego.

Mrs. Lowsky, walking her French poodle, sniffed. "When's that husband of yours coming back?"

"A week before Labor Day. He has school to teach."

"Why didn't you go with him?"

"I don't like heights." It was the truth. I avoided elevators and airplanes. I could not imagine spending an entire summer hiking across the Alps where my husband was, studying the quiet formations of rock, taking in research that he would use to compose a diary of remembrances long after our marriage was over.

One evening, as the sun frolicked in a pink and orange sky, Peter barbecued chicken on the deck in the backyard. I stretched out on the chaise longue in a skimpy summer frock dotted with white and yellow daisies. My exposed shoulders had tanned evenly over the past four weeks. Peter hummed and turned the chicken. The smoky charcoals hissed and sputtered with fat drippings. I closed my eyes and let my lungs fill with the smells of burned flesh.

"I'm sick of this weather," I said. "It makes me groggy."

"You seem to be enjoying it."

"Appearances don't mean anything. You know that."

"You mean Mrs. Lowsky? She thinks we're having an affair."

"Aren't we?" I squinted. The sun burst into a fiery nimbus around Peter's sleek body. His face darkened against the sunlight, and I wondered if he was smiling or frowning.

"I haven't kissed you," he said.

"But you want to. You've always wanted to."

"Everyone has his limits. Mine stop right there before a kiss."

"You don't have to kiss to be unfaithful. You can talk your way into anything."

"What are you trying to say to me?" Peter flipped the chicken onto a paper plate and walked into the steaming house. When he returned, he filled a bucket full of water and carried it over to the barbecue.

"Hey, stop. That's no way to put it out."

"You've got a better idea?"

"Let it burn itself out. How about an iced tea?"

Peter shrugged. "I'll get it."

I sipped the cool amber liquid and watched the smoke from the barbecue knit into hazy gauze. Peter hunkered over the patio table chewing corn on the cob. I sat across from him, gnawing on a chicken's wing. The distance between us widened, and from the living room, the telephone rang.

Peter rose and wiped his hands on a napkin. "I'll get it."

"Let it go to the machine." I grasped his wrist, tugging him back down, toward me. "You never know who it might be."

Our eyes locked, and for a moment, I thought I heard him mumble something about love.

"Are you finished with the grub?" he asked again.

I handed him my plate and followed him into the house. An invisible wall of heat crashed into me, bruising my chest, shoulders and face. I stumbled into the living room toward the flickering red light from the answering machine. I pressed the blue button and waited for the tape to rewind. A long beep preceded my husband's voice, cool, clear, refreshing, in the thick cottony swelter. "Trip's over early. I'll be home tomorrow. I'll call you from the airport. Love you."

When I turned around, Peter was standing before me. He pulled me into his arms and stroked my hair with his just-washed hands. My body relaxed into a sob until my arms shook and my chest ached. He held me tighter and tighter, not letting the force of my tears break me. I thought of the heat rising from the coals, the series of fires blazing in the dry fields around the highway, the barren desert of my heart, and the tumbleweed love of a husband I hardly recognized by his voice.

"It'll be all right," Peter whispered. "I'll come by and visit."

But already I could feel the coolness of an ending summer drift into the room from the large sliding glass window. I could feel its tempting relief snake around my ankles, tighten around my calves, seize my waist, pull me under its hypnotic spell. I imagined my days from this moment forward, coalescing into dense moisture that would extinguish any wildfire threatening to ravage the fragile terrain of my life. I saw Peter slipping into the distance, a fading star tumbling back into the sky, and for a long while, I let his hands warm against my back, and imagined the charcoal taste of his mouth against my lips, the kiss he could never give me reflected in his eyes.

Friends

In my bathroom there are two pictures taped to the mirror above the sink: one of Lenda Murray, the current Ms. Olympia, and one of Nora, my sister. On days I didn't want to work out, I stared at Nora's slim body. In the photo, Nora hugged a palm tree and winked at the camera. "God, it's hot in California," she said, afterward. "Do you think I could go for a drive?" Nora was 17, a high school senior from Nebraska with a full-tuition scholarship to Harvard in the fall. I kissed her cheek and handed her the keys to the Rabbit, not knowing she wouldn't come back, that the car would run out of gas, that her body would be found two states away in the back of a stripped camper shell, rotting from 110 degree desert heat, blood and semen crusting on her parted purple lips.

When I looked at that picture, I cupped a fist with my palm and caressed the knuckles, one by one. I whispered, softly, tenderly, "Nora, baby," before I slipped into a muscle shirt and shorts. I laced up my Nikes, ready to lift the weight of a grown man from my breasts.

On a Thursday night, I lay down on a black vinyl bench at Gold's Gym, closed my eyes, and curled my fingers around a bar stacked with 150-pound weights. My best friend and workout partner, Georgiana, stood above me, shadowing my grip. I inhaled and lifted the bar from its cradle. My chest tightened, and I saw Nora's killer, a bald vulture with rotten teeth, descend. I squeezed the bar and felt him tremble. Just before he touched my breasts, I exhaled and heaved him up. *One*, Georgiana counted. Again the killer descended, close enough for me to smell the whiskey on his breath, before I pushed him off me. Again, and again. On the tenth repetition, metal clicked against metal, and I opened my eyes. The killer was gone. Sweat dripped from my forehead.

"Not bad," Georgiana said. "You'll be able to raise that weight next week."

I sat up, swung my legs over the bench. I wiped my forehead and gulped a mouthful of water from a water bottle Georgiana handed me. "I want to be at 200 for the contest."

Georgiana shrugged. "I don't know if you can do it. That's an extra 50 pounds." Georgiana's gaze staggered off into the distance, and her face softened. "Hey, Stacey, check out the new aerobics instructor."

"Later. I want to do one more set." I wasn't here to ogle at women, though I sometimes found myself comparing the definitions of their biceps and the tone of their thighs in the locker room while I showered and dressed. Usually, Georgiana didn't notice them either. We were serious weight trainers, amateur hopefuls, and our five day a week excursion to Gold's Gym reflected our commitment to our bodies, our selves.

I thought about adding more weights, then changed my mind when I noticed Georgiana staring down the hall like a child entranced by the Pied Piper's song. I lay down on the bench and slid under the bar. "Pay attention and spot me, Juliet."

"Huh, oh, yeah." Georgiana cupped her hands outside my wide grip. After five repetitions, I called it quits.

"So, where's the instructor?" I asked.

"Huh, oh, yeah, the instructor." Georgiana's gaze trailed across the mirrored walls past the locker rooms and down the hall where dance music bounced. A woman's high pitched voice shouted, "One, two, three…"

We took a break, grabbed our water bottles, and sauntered toward the aerobics room. I didn't believe pounding my feet against a carpeted floor and throwing my arms over my head could be considered serious exercise. Sure, it accelerated the heartbeat and pumped blood into the extremities, but so did a good horror flick. It couldn't shape my body into the hard chiseled features I was looking for.

In the long, narrow room, Georgiana nodded toward a woman in pink leotards with a white cotton sweatband over her blond bangs. She smiled as she shouted instructions over the booming music. Her slender arms and legs sprung up and down with exuberant energy. Georgiana leaned against the doorjamb, a dreamy look in her brown eyes. The woman reminded me of a curious cheerleader I had dated in college, the one who said she wanted to try things out, the one I drove home only to discover she was Georgiana's steady a year before we met. Georgiana laughed when I told her. "She fooled you, too," she said.

"Almost, not quite. I'm sharper than you," I teased.

I tugged on Georgiana's damp muscle shirt. "Okay, enough, Juliet. She's not my type."

Georgiana crossed her arms and tossed her head. "Who says we're looking for you?" Georgiana – faithful confidante, listless dreamer – was not the same young woman I had met five years ago at a college bar. Formerly, a reed-thin runner whose bouts with anorexia eliminated her from competing nationally, she had over the years gained a hefty amount of weight along with a quiet self-confidence. I saw her sneaking glimpses at pretty women who passed our table on Friday nights, flirting with the teenage waitress who wore too much make-up, slathering too much butter on her dinner rolls, and chewing with her mouth open. She had cut her long brown curls into a stylish bob and had learned to swagger like a bad guy in an old western movie. I loved her the way you love a younger, irrepressible sister, unconditionally. And she loved me back in her careless, no-nonsense fashion which I had taken for granted as the years past. When I started working out two years ago, Georgiana joined me. We never discussed it. Good friends were like that, I guessed, close enough to almost read each other's thoughts.

I balled my hand into a fist and playfully nudged Georgiana in the ribs. "Let's go, Juliet."

Georgiana waved. "Go ahead and shower. I'll meet you here in ten minutes."

In the musty shower stall, I soaped up, feeling strange about Georgiana's sudden infatuation. As I toweled dried my short crop of hair and rubbed gel into the ends, I wondered about Georgiana's lapse in concentration as we worked out and speculated on how it might affect us. Weight training required alertness and dedication. Neither of us could afford a slip in either of them if we wanted to compete next year in the amateur competition as planned.

At the registration counter, I waited for Georgiana. Women and men with nylon gym bags signed in and out. I poked my head into the aerobics class, thinking she might still be in there. The instructor was bent over a portable stereo player changing the tape. Her high curved buttocks arched in the air, and a pang of longing startled me. I turned around and bumped into Georgiana's broad chest.

"Ah-ha, caught you, woman." A broad smile creased her tan face. "So, we agree, she's a ten."

"Seven and a half," I said, trying to be playful. "Her triceps are flabby and her hips are too broad."

"That's normal on a woman."

"Are you saying I'm not normal?"

Georgiana held open the door. We strolled into the parking lot. Hazy sunlight slanted across our backs. It was early fall, and I was looking forward to viewing the first football game of the season. Georgiana unlocked the passenger door to her old Dodge. "No, you're beyond normal." Georgiana squeezed my shoulder. "You're goddess of the free weights."

***

Two Sundays later, I arrived at Georgiana's apartment a little before noon, hoping to help her clean the dishes I knew would be in the sink, and tidy up the living room somewhat so we could actually sit on the couch. When Georgiana answered the door, her smile vanished. "Uh, Stacey, didn't you get my message?"

"What message?" I wedged my foot into the apartment before she could close the door. "Game isn't till one, right? I thought I'd come by early. Surprise you."

"Yeah, big surprise."

"Well, aren't you going to let your best friend in? Or am I going to have to watch the game through the window?"

Georgiana followed me into the living room. "Holy shit," I said. "What happened here? Did Mary Poppins drop in for a visit or what?"

No more Chinese take-out cartons or pizza boxes teetered on the coffee table like avant-garde sculptures. Someone had fluffed the pillows and neatly arranged them on the beige couch. The green carpet had been vacuumed and sprayed with the scent of wild flowers. Even the TV screen gleamed with our reflections.

The kitchen sink stared vacantly at me. The counters sparkled. I opened the refrigerator. Romaine lettuce, tomatoes, carrots, onions, mushrooms, and oranges filled the shelves instead of the usual ribs, milk, and a case of Michelob beer.

"What's come over you?" I asked, twisting the top off a bottle of mineral water. I leaned back on the couch, feeling the springiness of the cushions without a wad of newspaper and back issues of *Sports Illustrated* under my bottom.

Georgiana squatted on an armrest and clasped her hands, glancing anxiously at the door. "Listen, Stace, I have a visitor coming. I thought we could tape the game and watch it later. Maybe tomorrow night after work?"

"What? I can't believe you'd go through the trouble of cleaning your house and then boot me out. It doesn't make sense."

"I have a date. Linda's coming over."

"Linda who?"

"The aerobics instructor."

"You asked her on a date? I don't believe you. How could you cancel on me? Who the hell is this woman? Ms. Fitness U.S.A.?"

"Listen. I thought you'd understand. It's just one date."

"It's just one date? Like hell I understand. If you cancel this, what makes me think you won't cancel the Super Bowl? How am I supposed to trust you'll even show up at the gym?" I smacked my forehead, feigning inspiration. "Oh, well, of course, you'll show. You have to have an excuse to see Linda, right? You just won't pay attention when there's music in the other room. You'll let me lie there with a 150 pounds on my chest screaming for mercy."

"Stop it!" Georgiana slapped her palms against her thighs and stood up. "Listen. I don't get angry when you go out, so why can't you accept I have a date?"

"I never go out. And it's not just a date. You canceled on me. Me. You're oldest friend. Hell, I've never canceled anything. Not even when my mother was sick in the hospital. Not even when my sister died. Jeez, Georgiana, have some common sense. Friends, first, then lovers."

"She has kids. We're catching a matinee before dinner. The sitter's in high school— big exam tomorrow—and can't stay up late."

"How about next weekend?" I asked.

"They're going to Marine World. She said she wanted to get to know me first by myself. Didn't want to scare me off with her kids. I said, Sure, no problem. I left you the message last night. It's not my fault your roommate didn't give it to you. I'm sorry if I hurt your feelings. There'll be a next time."

"You're crazy."

"Crazy in love."

"Whatever."

Georgiana touched my knee. "Listen. I don't mean to be rude. You can stay for a bit. Just keep your feet off the coffee table. I just polished."

"Jeez, you *are* in love."

I crossed my arms over my chest and stared up at the cottage-cheese ceiling.

When Nora and I were little girls, we always thought the particles would fall into our eyes and make us cry. The sudden memory seized me, and I closed my eyes, hoping it would go away. A trickle of fear and loneliness seeped into my chest. I didn't want to argue: *maybe there won't be a next time.* How did I know? It might be just one date, and she'll be gone forever. Maybe Georgiana will hate her kids, or the dog will get sick. C'mon, Stacey, I told myself, let her go in peace. You'd want the same thing, right?

I opened my eyes, feigned a smile, and tried to be polite. "So, tell me about this Linda."

Georgiana's shoulders slacked and she nestled beside me on the couch. For a moment, Georgiana gazed off in the distance as if visualizing everything she knew of this woman she had asked out. "There's not much to tell," she said. "She's thirty-two, divorced, two kids, girl and boy, ten and seven, willing to settle down if the right woman shows up."

Georgiana gave me a sidelong glance, a sly way of letting me know she was thinking something she knew I wouldn't approve of, but couldn't help thinking anyway. I slapped her thigh and laughed. "You're hoping you're the right woman."

Georgiana shrugged. "It's too early to tell." The doorbell rang. "That's her. You'd better get going. Sorry about the game."

"No problem," I lied. "Just make sure it doesn't happen again. Old friends don't like to lose status, you know?" I jabbed her playfully in the ribs, gulped the rest of the mineral water, and placed the bottle on the coffee table. Georgiana gasped. She snatched the bottle and rubbed the ring of water with the edge of her T-shirt, then bolted for the door. Her close-set brown eyes twinkled like twin stars and her lips parted fully to reveal the crooked front teeth she hated to show. "Hello, Linda, you're looking lovely. Have you met my workout partner, Stacey Bennett?"

I offered Linda my hand. Her fingers were smooth and slim in my broad, veiny grasp. She looked like a greeting card angel with her blond hair exploding in a golden nimbus around her heart-shaped face. Our eyes met, and she smiled. A dimple pierced her left cheek. I held Linda's hand a moment too long. My throat constricted and my heart thumped wildly in my chest. "I'd better be going," I said. I squeezed between them to get out the door. I kept my eyes on the pavement. My voice was scarcely a whisper. "See you Monday at the gym," I said to Georgiana.

For a moment after Georgiana had closed the door, I stood listlessly in the breezeway with the early afternoon air souring around me. The fog had burned off, but the sky was overcast. Thick gray clouds hunkered down against my shoulders, casting a shadowy gloom over my thoughts. I dragged my feet across the cracked pavement and shut the door of my black Bronco, feeling safe in the cool interior. I rolled down the window and stared at the parked cars, wishing I had never come.

The emptiness I had avoided since Nora's death washed over me, drowning me in a swirl of emotions. Working out with Georgiana had eased the burden of guilt I had felt in giving Nora my car keys, thinking she'd be safe, believing she'd come home.

Every Friday night after our workout, Georgiana and I met at Iggy's Sports Bar. We talked about work—Georgiana clerked part-time at a local video store while dickering around in school, still trying to settle on a major, and I taught eighth grade physical education and coached a girl's softball team in the summer. Sometimes we'd talk about other things in our lives, what little there was left of them. Even in Georgiana's company, I never forgot Nora. Sometimes after too many beers, I'd start blabbing about how wonderful Nora had been. Nora had volunteered as a candy striper at the hospital, helping patients recover from surgery. She had trusted people, and had lived by her motto, Never judge, especially after I had told her I like women. Georgiana would listen sympathetically and pat my hand. Then she'd remind me of how each year I'd scout for a skinny girl with two left feet or a fat girl with glasses, and how I'd take them under my wing and coach them even though they had no real hope of becoming athletes. "You have compassion, like Nora," she'd say. What I had never confessed to Georgiana was that I thought by mentoring those awkward girls I could make it up to Nora, somehow, someway. But every year, when those girls graduated and left for high school, I was bereft.

A few minutes later, I spied Georgiana and Linda leaving in Georgiana's old Dodge. They were smiling and laughing at some private joke. Long after they had left, I turned the key in the ignition and revved the engine. Once Georgiana and I had discussed what we would do if either of us found a girlfriend, but that was three years ago, and the talk had been light-hearted, far from serious. Georgiana confessed to being shy, and now that I was training, I had no time for romance. Seeing Georgiana leave with Linda left me feeling numb like I had at Nora's funeral. The reality struck me as odd, out of place, almost impossible. A date? Somehow, in spite of my grief and anger, I'd always imagined I'd be first.

At home, I decided not to watch the game. Instead, I phoned my 65-year-old mother in Nebraska. Cecilia and I had never been close, she was always too conservative and outspoken, and I was too edgy and forlorn to care about the things she cared for: gardening, cooking, and chitchatting with neighbors. I moved to California to attend the University of California, Berkeley, and settled nearby after graduation. When Nora died, I flew out for a week, but didn't stay. I couldn't bear the pale pink walls, the lace curtains, the teddy bears and the posters of Van Halen in my sister's room, the room we had shared before I had moved to California. Mom tried to persuade me to retire downstairs in the guestroom, but everywhere I turned, I'd see my sister's long dirty blond hair, her slender arms, her fragile legs. I'd smell her apricot skin in the pies Mom baked and hear her tangy laughter in the wind rustling outside the window. For twenty-two hours I slipped from room to room, dodging Nora's ghost, until I packed my bags and left, heavy from guilt and fear and longing. I never came back.

I looked up Cecilia's phone number in my red address book and dialed the number.

"Hello?" My mother's voice cracked into a cough, a remnant of thirty years of smoking. I imagined her seated in a wide armchair in the living room dressed in a floral housecoat with her gray hair bundled high on her head and a dash of rosy lipstick streaked across her narrow lips. Beside her, a second cup of coffee cooled and static crackled from a portable radio tuned to an obnoxious talk show.

"Mom, it's Stacey. In California."

"Why haven't you visited?"

"I've been busy."

"For three years? Have you heard about the Wilsons?"

"No, I didn't call to hear about the neighbors. I wanted to talk to you."

"About what?"

"Just talk, Mom. Can't we just talk?"

"Humph. You never wanted to talk. You said I was too hog stubborn and pigeon minded. Like I've always said, you're too big for Nebraska. But I suppose you're happy."

I twirled the phone cord and thought of Georgiana dating Linda. "Pretty much, I guess. I've been working out a lot. I'm going to compete, bring home a medal, just like I did in high school, remember?"

My mother coughed, then cleared her throat. "Don't suppose you'd like to come visit this year. The Stewarts will be celebrating Thanksgiving with their grandkids and they've invited me, but I'd rather stay home and cook my own dinner, if you know what I mean. It'd be mighty nice if you'd come and visit. Bring a girlfriend, if you'd like."

It was a generous offer, coming from my mother, the woman who threatened me with passages of Sodom and Gomorrah when she caught me kissing Jenny Stewart in the backyard when I was in high school.

"I'll have to think about it," I said, lowering my voice.

"I've redecorated. You could stay in your old room."

"Why don't you come to California? I have a big kitchen."

"Too much skin," Mom quipped.

The silence between us widened. I thought of my sister's hair floating down the banister, cascading over the table cloth, lighting the air with a subtle perfume. And then I thought of my mother, alone, since Nora died, sitting around a table with neighbors who cared more about her than I did, the only living relative who seldom called and never wrote.

"You weren't this way when your daddy died," Mom said.

"Daddy wasn't murdered."

"It ain't your fault, sweetheart." Mom's rough voice softened. "How many times must I say it? No one blamed you."

My fingers gripped the cord too tightly. The knuckles glowed white. "I'll think about it and let you know," I said.

Six weeks later, Georgiana was still dating Linda. She arrived early at the gym for Linda's five-thirty aerobics class, then plunged into weightlifting with me at six-thirty. At first, I didn't say anything. Georgiana was a grown woman, and if she thought she could handle two workouts, then she probably could. Only her stamina had diminished steadily over those six weeks, and I found it nearly impossible to challenge her.

"C'mon, Georgie, one more set. You need to lift more than that if you want to compete next year." It was Thursday night at the gym and we were finishing up our arm workout. Georgiana had only completed two lightweight sets. I stood beside her, watching her elbows tremble each time she lowered the weight.

Georgiana released the dumbbells and wiped the sweat from her forehead. "We need to talk," she said.

"Later." I grabbed two twenty-pound dumbbells and straddled the black vinyl bench in front of the mirrors. I shouted over the loud rock and roll music piped in through the speakers. "You need to spot me, first."

Georgiana returned the fifteen-pound weights to their cradles, one at a time. There was preciseness to her movements that I interpreted as frailty, an almost too exacting cautiousness that had only surfaced since her aerobic workouts with Linda.

"I'm not competing," Georgiana said.

I stopped in mid-set. "Why not? Did Linda tell you not to?"

"No, I've been meaning to tell you for some time."

"How long?"

"Five weeks."

"So, why are you bringing it up now? What's changed?"

"I need to graduate and get a *real* job. I'm almost thirty and I'm living like a teenager!" Georgiana stared at me. "I can't do it, Stacey. I can't see myself working out five days a week anymore. It's insane. I need to get my life together."

I set the dumbbells on the weight rack and gazed at Georgiana's reflection. The void I had ignored when Nora had died flooded into my veins again. I glanced away from Georgiana's reflection and stared at the blue rivers of blood beneath my skin. I flexed my arm, and the rivers surged. When I spoke, my voice bristled with despondent anger. "First, Friday nights, now workouts. Next you'll be telling me to forget the games. What will that leave us?"

Georgiana shrugged. "Can't we still be friends?"

"What about Linda? What does she think of us?"

"She's cool about it. She knows you're not interested in me."

I felt the walls of privacy I had built crumble around me. "What else did you tell her?"

"I said you live to workout. That's all you seem to care about anymore."

"That's not true." My throat constricted. My hands clenched. Beads of perspiration dripped down my forehead and stung my eyes. "That's not all I care about and you know it. I care about lots of other things. Things I thought you cared about, too, but I was wrong. All wrong." I snatched my water bottle and towel and trotted toward the locker rooms.

"Stacey, wait. You're not going to let this destroy us, are you?"

"That's not for me to decide, Juliet. I'm not the one in love, remember?"

Georgiana touched my shoulder. "Listen, Stacey, I've been thinking. Maybe you could come over to Linda's for Thanksgiving. That way neither one of us has to be alone. What do you say?"

I folded my arms across my chest and frowned. "Forget it," I said. "Just leave me alone."

I stalked into the locker room, stripped, and lay naked in the dry sauna. A few minutes later, the door cracked open and Linda stepped in with a towel hugged around her breasts. She smiled when she noticed me. "Aren't you Georgiana's partner?"

"Was."

"I'm sorry, but I forgot your name."

"Stacey." I closed my eyes and rolled my head toward the ceiling. Steam rose off the pores of my skin and hissed like the dry coals.

Linda seated herself on the bench below me and arranged her hair into a knot above her head so that her long hair wouldn't brush against my arm. "How long have you and Georgiana been friends?"

"Five years." *And I ended up taking a backseat to you in only six weeks.*

"Georgiana tells me you're planning on competing next year." Linda's voice was modulated like a schoolteacher's.

I grunted. I didn't want to talk about it. There was nothing to talk about anymore.

"I teach a morning class at Fifth Street," Linda explained. "And I hear there's this girl named Erika who's looking for a partner. She's competed before and won a state title. I hear she's a good person to workout with. If you'd like, I'll get her phone number for you."

I rolled onto my side and opened my eyes. "Did Georgiana put you up to this?" I asked. "Because if she did, the answer's no."

"I haven't seen Georgiana since class. I only mentioned it because I know how much potential you have, and working out with Georgiana's not going to get you where you want to go." Linda propped one leg on the bench and leaned her head beside my arm. A dreamy smile appeared on her face. "I was only thinking about you on the cover of one of those fitness magazines," she said. "You're built like a winner."

"Thanks." It was the best compliment I had received in my life.

"Think about it," Linda said. "I'd love to help." A strand of hair fell from her head and brushed my shoulder. My skin tingled, electrified by the unexpected touch. I saw Nora kissing my cheek, saying good-bye to me. A wall of reserve lowered and I felt damaged and alone. Linda gazed at me with solemn concern and I realized how easily it must have been for Georgiana to fall in love with her. Feeling more exposed than naked, I climbed down the bench and wrapped a towel around my breasts.

"Will you think about it?" Linda asked, her voice gently insistent.

I gripped the handle of the door, afraid to turn around and surrender to hope. "Yes, I'd like the help," I said. "Very much."

Next Sunday, I brought a bag of tortilla chips and salsa to Georgiana's apartment as a gift of atonement for my brash display of anger during the week. When Georgiana greeted me at the door, she pushed back a mop of dark curls from her forehead and straightened the belt of her bathrobe. "I'm sorry," I said, offering up the gifts. "Friends?"

"You should have called," Georgiana said.

"Now what?"

"Linda's kids went off to visit their dad this weekend and Linda spent the night."

"I see." My voice wavered with understanding. I handed her the bag of tortilla chips and salsa. "Enjoy."

"Stacey, you aren't mad again, are you?"

I shook my head. Faint humming floated down the hall. A light wispy voice asked, "Georgiana, who's there?"

"It's Stacey. I forgot about the game."

"Well, let her in. We can all watch it."

Linda snuggled up against Georgiana's back and pecked her neck. Her eyes gleamed with happiness when she gazed at me. I marveled at her generosity, first in finding me a workout partner, and now, in inviting me to intrude upon an otherwise intimate weekend. And then I imagined her bare arms and legs tangled in the sheets of Georgiana's single bed, the warm smell of lust rising from her skin, the delicate tenderness of her touch.

"No, thank you," I said, blushing at my thoughts. "Maybe some other time."

***

Erika was exactly the training partner I needed. In two weeks, my lats gained a quarter of an inch. A week later I noticed more musculature in my thighs and calves. A sculpture was slowly emerging from the bulk of my body. I turned from side to side, posing in the full-length mirror in the locker room, admiring the gains.

"Nice abs."

I spun around and glimpsed Linda bent over her tennis shoes. "I didn't think anyone noticed."

"I do," Linda said. "I'm a mother, and mothers notice everything."

"How are your kids doing?" I asked, trying to be friendly.

"Fine. They seem to really like Georgiana. Melissa's asked her to come to her soccer game next weekend and Jude wants her to help him construct a Lego city." Linda zipped her bag and tossed it into the locker. The metal door clicked shut. "Georgiana tells me she invited you over for Thanksgiving. I'm hoping you'll come."

"I don't want to be a bother," I said, blushing.

"If you were bothersome, I'd ask you to leave."

I smiled; she was serious.

Linda knotted her long blond hair into a ponytail. I thought of Nora's hair, of how I'd brush and braid it down her back. My fingers twitched with the memory. How long had it been since I touched a woman? Any woman? Two years? Three? It was hard to keep track of things anymore. Georgiana was right. Only my body mattered. Making it hard, chiseled, like stone. I wanted to show the world there was no such thing as a weak woman. But watching Linda pull her hair from her face reminded me of my loneliness, of how I had let only two things fill the void in my life since Nora had died: my friendship with Georgiana and weight training. Suddenly, I felt out of focus.

Linda swept her bangs back with an elastic headband and straightened the straps of her black leotard. "I cook a mean turkey, and I know how to make low-fat mashed potatoes and stuffing." Linda smiled and squeezed my hand. "I wouldn't ask if I didn't want you over."

I glanced down at my feet. "I'll let you or Georgiana know," I said.

After Linda left, I squatted on a bench beside the metal lockers. Water hissed from the showers. Blow dryers buzzed. Steam and perspiration evaporated in a thin mist above my head. I dabbed my lips with a towel, wondering why I ached all over, my skin branded by Linda's inviting touch.

I didn't return Georgiana's phone call that night or the night after. Something in me froze when I heard her voice. I wanted to confess the growing crush I had on Linda without threatening Georgiana, or straining whatever friendship we had left between us. Before Georgiana's romance with Linda, I had dreamed every night of Nora's murderer circling the Volkswagen Rabbit with his Harley motorcycle. His eyes stalked my sister's slender, unsuspecting form as she rolled down the window, letting her elbow rest on the ledge, with the wind sweeping through her long dirty blond hair. Sometimes a light burned in the distance, the color of fire and ashes, a summer sunset in the desert. Then the Volkswagen's engine sputtered and wheezed. The car stalled. Alone. No one to rescue Nora but the man on the Harley, descending slowly, a vulture waiting for his prey to die.

But lately, those dreams had been replaced by images of Linda and Georgiana and I, of the three of us holding hands, walking through the park, pointing at the starlings. Linda walked between us, her slim body swaying under a loose knit dress. Linda tilted her head back to kiss Georgiana, then she turned and offered those same lips to me. I leaned forward and closed my eyes, feeling the tenderness of her mouth over mine, the gentle probing of her tongue between my teeth, the jolt of energy tingling from her fingers as they held my hand, suffusing me with an unbearable desire. I gasped and woke with my legs twisted in the rumpled sheets. A cool prickly sensation inched across my scalp, a shiver of guilt and fear, longing and more longing, dissolving into sorrow.

The phone rang.

I leaned back against the damp pillow and listened to the answering machine. Georgiana repeated the same message she had already left. "Are you coming to see the game this weekend? Call me if you are. And don't forget about Thanksgiving. We hope you'll decide to join us. It should be fun."

Fun. Whenever was a love triangle described as being fun? I rolled over, cupped my hands under my cheek and closed my eyes, trying to fall back to sleep. I didn't want to have to deal with any of this; I didn't want to imagine what Georgiana might have to say.

On Monday night, I skipped my workout with Erika, telling her I wasn't feeling well, and headed over to Iggy's Sports Bar, a place Georgiana and I frequented. The bartender was an older man, balding with a swipe of gray-streaked hair brushed over the scalp to hide the loss. His crooked black eyebrows looked like they'd been squiggled on by a child's hand. One eye squinted as he filled glasses with people's drowning dreams. I sidled up to the counter beside the TV and ordered a beer. The bartender smiled out of recognition and said, "The first one's on me, sweetie."

I grimaced and gulped the first two mouthfuls. I glanced over the crowd of men in silver-studded leather jackets, women in denim jeans and clingy knit tops, and wondered why Georgiana and I started coming here in the first place. A hefty man seated himself beside me and grunted as he slurped the froth from his beer.

I said nothing.

When I watched the game with Georgiana, we spoke of the team's past records, of what players we favored, and who might win tonight's game. We nudged each other whenever we were wrong about a move and cheered together at each touchdown. Our laughter permeated the thin walls, and sometimes her roommate, a surly engineering student, left the apartment to study in the backseat of her car. After the game, we lounged around among discarded pizza boxes, bags of half-eaten pretzels, and crushed beer cans, our one indulgence of the week. I wondered if Georgiana was watching the game with Linda. I imagined them snuggling against each other, their lips murmuring sweet nothings during commercials.

People cheered and whooped and hollered. I glanced at the TV and saw my life for what it was: a replay of a fumbled pass.

During half time, the bartender tried to make conversation. I retreated to a booth by the jukebox. I tried to imagine what my days would be like now. Pictures from my old life before Georgiana, which I simply thought of as a series of meaningless clips with random order, played in my head. I saw Nora lounging beside me on the couch, telling me how much she hated football, all those punts and charges and silly butt pats. "Ice skating's better," she'd say, tossing back her hair. "If I had your coordination, I would have been an ice skater." She slumped beside me, her head against my shoulder, drifting into sleep. I stroked her hair, unaware of the troubles that lay before us.

I drained my beer and stroked the sides of the empty mug. My mother was right. It wasn't my fault Nora had died, just like it wasn't my fault Georgiana had fallen in love with Linda. I had spent the last few years thinking I could shape the past and mold the future the way I had with my body, through discipline and control. Now I saw myself as I was, a lonely single woman in a sports bar, pining over the memory of her sister and clinging to a five-year friendship that no longer fit.

Maybe working out at a different gym would change things. Already Erika had improved my technique, increasing my chances of placing in a local competition. Who knows? If I hunkered down and devoted myself completely to fitness, then maybe Monday night football wouldn't mean so much anymore, and I could let go of Georgiana, of whatever there was left between us.

***

The next day I went directly from work to the gym. Already, the converted warehouse was crowded with men and women cycling and rowing, pressing and squatting. Music boomed from the aerobics room down the hall. I changed quickly, warmed up five minutes on the bike, and joined Erika by the free weights.

An hour later, Georgiana appeared from the aerobics room, exhausted and sweaty. Her bulky body struggled to jog around moving bodies in bright Lycra and oversized sweatshirts. She waved, and I pretended not to see her. "Why are you avoiding me?" Georgiana asked.

I set the dumbbells in their cradles and waved to Erika to take a break. I sat down on a black vinyl bench and motioned for Georgiana to sit beside me. She shook her head. "I'd rather go for a walk. For privacy," she said.

I grumbled, excused myself to ask Erika if she'd mind cutting our workout two sets short, and then trotted over to Georgiana. "Let's go. I'll come back to shower," I said.

Outside, the cool air accosted me. I shivered under my sweatshirt and Georgiana offered me her jacket. I declined.

"Why haven't you returned my calls?" Georgiana asked.

"I've been too busy training."

"Every day, all day, for the last week?"

I shoved my fists into the pockets of my sweatshirt and kept my eyes on the shadows thrown by the amber streetlights. "Yeah, I was. Sorry."

"Sorry? What happened to 'friends, first, then lovers'?"

"I was wrong. You need your space, and you have your own life. It isn't in my place to interfere. Friends have boundaries, you know?"

"And not returning phone calls accounts for one of them? I don't think so. Something else is going on, and you're not telling me."

"I don't need to tell you everything."

"You used to." Georgiana's voice quivered. She coughed and feigned a scratch in her throat. "We told each other everything. Good and bad. No judgments, remember?"

"Yeah, well, we were young and stupid."

"It wasn't that long ago." Georgiana pinched my arm above the elbow. She stopped walking and pulled me toward her, though I tried to maneuver my face so she couldn't see the tears brimming in my eyes, the ones I knew I couldn't let fall. For a long moment she stared at me, like I was something she had found again and was afraid of losing. Then she tried to fold me in her arms, but I shoved her away.

"It's about Linda, isn't it?" she said. "You still don't like her."

"Like? What's there to like? She's a woman for chrissakes, and you're in love with her. Big deal. Can we just drop it? I'm tired of fighting with you. Go in peace and love Linda, okay?"

"What about us?" Georgiana asked, her hands on my shoulders. "We're too good of friends to let this come between us."

"It already has. And there's nothing you can do about it, okay? Trust me. It'll be better for us not seeing each other. In fact, I'm thinking about moving to the gym downtown. I hear they have more free weights."

"Why are you doing this, Stacey? There has to be something else you're not telling me."

"There's nothing," I lied. "Nothing." My voice trailed off in a whisper. A swirl of leaves danced around our ankles. I shivered. Georgiana wrapped her arms around me, and I didn't think quick enough to pull back this time. Her thick body was warm through her coat. A car drove by flashing its garishly bright headlights over us. I didn't want to tell her, but I felt she had a right to know. "I think I'm falling in love . . . with Linda," I murmured into her collar.

"I don't blame you. She's a wonderful woman," Georgiana said.

"That's why I won't return your calls, and that's why I can't accept the invitation to Thanksgiving dinner. I don't want my feelings to interfere more than they already have."

"But can't we all be friends?" she asked.

I eased away from the warmth of Georgiana's body. A gulf of cold air swept down between us, rattling the leaves on the half-naked sycamores. I swayed forward. My gaze rested on Georgiana's face. "Maybe someday when I have a girlfriend, we can all be friends," I said, "but right now, things won't work."

Georgiana was silent.

I shifted through my mind, searching for a better explanation. "Remember when my sister died?" I said. "There was something you told me, something so profound, I thought you'd read it out of some damn psycho-babble book? You said I had to let go and get on with my life. Well, that's where we are now. I'm not saying it's easy—the Goddess knows it hasn't been—but it's something we need to do."

Georgiana shoved her fists into her front pockets and kicked at the crisp, newly fallen leaves. "And if I stop seeing Linda?"

"For chrissakes, Georgie, I'm not asking you to stop seeing Linda. She's a kind woman. Generous. She goes out of her way to help people she doesn't really know. I don't know if she told you, but that's how I found Erika. It was her idea. She said I had potential I wasn't using. Now I'm finally training the way I need to win. I'm happy. And you're happy. Isn't that enough?"

Georgiana arched one eyebrow. And though the hope in her eyes persisted, she whispered, "I guess it'll have to be."

I braced my arms over my chest and raised my eyes toward the heavens. I picked the brightest star in the sky and imagined it was Nora smiling down at me. I thought of the changes I was going to make: to concentrate on my workouts, to visit my mother for Thanksgiving, and maybe to start dating. I breathed in deeply. My skin tingled with the refreshing change of fall to winter. This time next year, I hoped to be sporting my first bodybuilding medal. And maybe, in a few years, I'd find a woman who could appreciate me as much as I did her. I slipped one arm around Georgiana's back. "Let's go," I said. "You can't keep Linda waiting."

Out of Focus

I'm standing outside the Mouse Trap in the rain, waiting for Jen to feed the meter. My long black hair whips around my face and neck, dangerously wet and heavy. Tony, the bouncer, sits astride a high-backed chair under the awning, smoking. The cool moist air works magic on his pale skin, making him glow like a lava lamp, soft and warm and comforting on this late January evening in the final year of my father's life. I wink at him, and he smiles. "Just threw a man out for hustling a lady," he says. "Blood, guts, and glory; all in a day's work."

I take a puff from his cigarette. The smoke sears my lungs like a long silver blade dividing my breath in two. I cough and try to smile at the same time, an impossible thing to do, and Tony laughs. "You, too? How long has it been? Three weeks?"

"Four months." I say it loudly, a banner of pride covering the misfortunate things I have done, including sleeping with my sister's boyfriend, a thing I will never tell no matter who asks.

Jen links her arm around mine and Tony's eyes caress her. Since the birth of her son, Jen's lost forty pounds from not eating. She runs three miles every day with the baby in a stroller, slicing the air away from her life. Afterward, she slips into a soft knit top and hip-hugging denim and paints her face in shades of fire and gold, a triumphant woman. She brags about the baby fat she's lost, the sleepless nights that calm her nerves, the full and tender breasts that leak when men touch them. Jen was embarrassingly fat since childhood; I'm truly impressed with her discipline, her focus. I've never been fat, only thin and anemic, and the only vice I've tried to kick has kicked me back. I don't bother trying to be good anymore. At twenty-five, it's not worth it.

We take a seat at a booth beside the bar and place our order with the clerk, a blond pony-tailed woman who chomps gum and pushes her bangs out of her eyes. "A beer and a coffee, black," I say. Jen leans forward and opens her pocket notebook on the scarred table and licks the tip of her ballpoint pen to get it to write.

Smoke, hair spray, and cheap aftershave shroud us through the dimly lit pool hall. Nirvana's "Heart-Shaped Box" plunks its sad serenade from the ancient jukebox. College boys with London Fog raincoats and new sneakers play against truckers and construction workers with long hair and stained T-shirts. They take turns leaning over the green velvet pool tables, contemplating their moves. The balls click and scatter like frightened children running home to dinner.

I rummage through my purse looking for some change to buy a package of cigarettes from the vending machine by the restrooms. When I return to the booth, the waitress has brought our drinks, beer for me, coffee for Jen. I watch her stir a packet of fake sugar into the dark fathomless pool. She puckers her lips and sips. I light a cigarette, try to inhale without choking this time. Can't. My lungs contract and lodge themselves in the base of my throat like angry fists.

Jen hates our father and would like to kill him but she's writing a book first. "Non-fiction," she tells me. "Nothing but the facts." I roll my eyes, remembering the words of our father, *Stop telling stories.* My sister, Jen, never spoke lies like we did. She wrote them down on slips of paper, folded them into threes, and slipped them under our bedroom door at night. There were stories of child-eating weeds, romances between celestial beings, plots to overthrow Smokey the Bear from a nationally televised campaign. My sister, Jen, thinks fiction is fact, fact is fiction. Growing up in our household, I can't blame her for the confusion. Everything was a bit out of focus.

"What about the time you didn't make it on the cheerleading team?" Jen asks.

"I made the cheerleading team, but I wanted to be on the debate team. They said I was too short to reach the microphone. I'm not tall like you. That's why I have to be bad, you know. It's not easy getting attention when you're short."

"Too short and soft spoken for the cheers," Jen writes. "Consoles herself with dating a tall man on the debate team."

I crush my cigarette in the golden ashtray and gulp down my beer.

"And what about your first kiss?"

"It was with Billy Irish in home ec. We were pretending to be the proud parents of a ten pound sack of flour we had to take with us everywhere, even to the movies. We just had a fight about who was going to take the flour home over the weekend, and I punched Billy in the stomach for knocking me up. 'I don't have a life,' I said. 'I've never been kissed.' That's when he plastered a wet one on my lips to shut me up so we wouldn't be suspended. Not exactly romantic, but it was my first."

"Tongued by a monkey trainer at the zoo while babysitting the neighbor's brat," Jen writes. "Comes home singing the theme song from *Planet of the Apes.* Starts dressing like a cave woman in lots of torn leather. Lets the perm grow out of her stringy black hair. Forgets how to use a fork. Love sick."

I slam the empty beer mug on the table. "I thought you were writing non-fiction."

"I'm compiling information to form a prototype of the late twentieth century woman. My first subject failed me."

"Who was that?"

"Our mother."

I nod, order a double shot of tequila, and gulp it down. Tony saunters into the pool hall, flexing his muscles. I wave for him to join us, but he shakes his head and takes a seat at the bar. He orders a soda and glances back at us, at my sister, who scribbles copiously in her pocket notebook.

I leave to go talk to him at the bar. "What's up?" I ask, crossing my arms on the polished counter and leaning forward so my breasts swell in my shirt.

Tony nurses his soda without noticing my cleavage. "Who's that chick?" He flicks his head back, slyly, as if the information is top secret.

"My sister."

"No shit?" He flashes a crooked smile and sidles up to the table where my sister scribbles. "Hey, how about going out sometime?"

Jen glances up, returns his smile.

"She's married with a kid and another on the way," I say, sitting down.

When he's gone, Jen slaps my hand. "How could you lie to him?"

I shrug. "The truth's boring."

"Nothing is more fascinating than the truth," Jen says, gathering her pocket notebook and heading for the door where Tony stands, his eyes smoldering like the tips of cigarettes.

Queen of Jingle Junk

Dana filled the electric teakettle, emptied a pouch of instant oatmeal into a bowl, boiled the water, set the bowl on the kitchen table, poured the water into the bowl and stirred with a plastic baby spoon. All the while, fourteen-month-old Joey rolled around on the living room carpet as she read a scary article in *Intervention* that said children who do not crawl have problems learning how to read and write, among other things. It quoted Dr. Norton, who described four children who'd been unable to master simple multiplication and then underwent six months of intensive four-point crawling only to sky-rocket from third-grade-level mathematics to pre-algebra.

The doctor said that some children recommended crawling indoors to prevent embarrassment from other children and unsympathetic adults. Other children suggested they crawl only when their parents weren't at home. But all the children in the study agreed that daily crawling, anywhere from fifteen to twenty minutes, had remarkably improved their learning ability and increased their self-esteem.

Dana's son, Joey, had never crawled. Whenever he wanted something, he'd roll onto his side and reach for it with his left arm extended, fingers outstretched. If he couldn't grasp the object, he'd roll onto his back and scoot forward by arching his shoulders and thrusting with his feet. Evidently, according to the article, Dana would have to enroll Joey in physical therapy if he was ever going to balance a checkbook. She glanced at Joey rocking from side to side on his back, hands clasped behind his head, a smile on his round face. Is this crawling business silly? she wondered, and yet Joey was the only child she knew who, at fourteen months, had not even attempted to move forward or backward on his belly.

The article jumped to page 22. Mike M., a ten-year-old boy, crawled intensively for thirteen months before he could stare at a page without having letters transpose. In the adjoining column was a side bar about a mother, six years older than Dana. The mother had been arrested for drowning her twenty-two-month-old daughter who had been diagnosed with cerebral palsy. Mercy killing, the mother was quoted as saying. A passerby jumped into the bay in an attempt to revive the child but a swift current pulled the girl downstream. The father of the child had been too angry to give interviewers comments. Dana wondered what her husband, Norman, would say if she had been the one accused of drowning Joey because he hadn't crawled yet. She imagined he'd tell reporters his wife never recovered from postpartum depression. Or maybe he'd say she was angry because she had postponed a stellar career as a corporate executive so she could stay home and nurse their son. The loneliness of child rearing in an adult community forced her to temporarily lose her mind. That, and all the nonsense reading, he'd say.

Phantom fantasies of imagined childhood disabilities in her son seemed like a big price to pay for reading a newspaper. But, the paper had been there on the doorstep. Dana didn't want it to blow away down the block, fifty pages flapping across the well-kept lawns of the older residents of Shady Oaks. She opened it and out came a barrel of trash to fill up her mind.

Joey rolled onto his side and rubbed his eyes. The house feels tired, too, even the furniture, exhausted from old marital battles. The latest fight ended with Dana recommending that Norman take a room at the Quicksleeper Inn where he worked as a night auditor. "It comes with the job, why waste it?" she said. And Norman, being the practical, no-nonsense, listen-to-your-wife, '90s guy, hasn't been home since he took Dana's advice. He packed his three sets of clean underwear, four white T-shirts, two gray slacks, one white shirt, black socks, and a red-and-blue striped necktie. The house hasn't been cleaned since he left last Friday.

Dana was the executive vice president for Jingle Junk mail ordering before becoming Joey's mother. She never developed the skills needed to vacuum, dust, launder and fold. She learned how to cook Chinese and Italian cuisine because it only required chopping, stirring, steaming and boiling—things she had learned when Norman prepared dinner for entertaining Dana's prospective clients. For example, the couple who developed the all-in-one-utensil. It was a fork, knife and spoon that folded into a nail clipper. It was listed for the dirt-cheap price of $9.95, plus shipping and handling. California residents had to add 7.5 percent sales tax. But that, Dana sighed, felt like a lifetime ago.

Now, Dana misses the deadlines and trumped-up ad copy she ran in the monthly Jingle Junk mail-order magazine. She misses the quirky staff of gum-chewing, booger-picking, loud-mouth wannabe writers and artists who whittled away eight to ten hours a day trying to creatively sell two hundred fifty thousand plastic neon-pink-and-green stamp-licking cows made in China.

Norman never understood Dana's obsession with Jingle Junk. He thought that her need to dominate over a staff of fifteen dubiously gifted prose liars was trashy and sophomoric, but then he thought that about all of Dana's professional career in the mail-order industry. Dana had written ad copy for a farm of sea monkeys who spontaneously reproduce every 24 hours and glow in the dark like tiny stars and then fizzle out and die once the water's changed. It was an advertisement so witty, people practically jumped out of their Easy Boys to grab their portable phones and dial the 1-800 number listed at the bottom of the television screen. Twenty-five telephone operators lost their voices in one week and a new batch of sixty-seven was hired to take orders. But to Norman, the ad was another in a string of strange embarrassments that was their marriage. Norman had, while Dana wrote about sea monkeys and other useless stuff, put himself through the university and graduated as a certified public accountant. But just when Norman thought he was going to net $50,000 to $60,000 a year, the job market for accountants crashed and the demand for Dana's slick ad copy boomed. Dana was offered $180,000 in 1992 to write a thirty-second ad for Black Tar Hair Cream with vegetable oil.

Despite her success, Dana wasn't satisfied. "You're twenty-nine," Norman said. "Maybe we should have children."

"But I don't need children. I create with words," Dana said.

"And I create with numbers. Either way you look at it, it's a lonely life. One little person might spice it up."

"So, have an affair," Dana suggested, half jokingly.

Norman frowned. "That's not what I meant and you know it."

"But what about my career?"

"It can wait. You can be Queen of Jingle Junk later."

"Fine. If that's how you feel about it, then screw me."

And he did.

Nine months and ten days later, Joey was born.

Dana never prepared herself to be a mother, so she called up Martha, her mother, for advice. Martha was a homemaker who still pulled her gray hair into a low bun and secured it with plastic-coated bobbie pins and a black net. She rolled pie crust and baked gingerbread men six hours a day. When Dana called, Martha had to excuse herself to turn down the oven to 325 degrees or else the bread would burn and, goodness knows, it's no fun eating burnt banana bread. "I don't know what to do," Dana said, a sobbing Joey in the background.

"Open your blouse and feed him," Martha said. "Check his diaper to make sure he's not wet. Throw him over your shoulder and pat his back. Boys get a lot of gas," she said. "And if that doesn't work, sing loud till your voice cracks."

Dana drew in a deep breath and closed her eyes. She wasn't expecting that type of advice, but she didn't know where she'd get any better help than from a woman who raised four dirt-eating, feet-stomping, hair-pulling girls and boys in a period spanning twenty years. It was a busy life being a mother. Dana thinks of the lonely woman sitting in the filthy apartment all day watching *Charlie's Angels*, drinking Pepsi, and munching on Lay's potato chips, waiting for her truck-driving husband to come home and tell her how many miles he covered and how many women he met along the way. It depressed Dana to think her mother's life could amount to that little after the woman had given so much.

When Dana was seventeen, she graduated with honors, enrolled at the junior college and vowed to pursue an exciting career as a foreign correspondent. She met Norman in a Laundromat when she was trying to decide whether or not to bleach the darks or the lights. Norman offered to help her and she watched him sort her clothes with the skill and grace she imagined only her mother had. Afterward, he asked her out for dinner—his house, homemade—and Dana fell in love with his chicken alfredo. Dana transferred to the university, received her bachelor's and immediately found work as a copy editor for a local fashion magazine. She and Norman eloped a week after *Flash Forward* printed her article on Lycra leggings.

It took Dana four years to write her way to a top-paying position with Jingle Junk as senior ad copyist. The following year, she was promoted to executive vice president. Then she became a mother.

Having Joey awakened Dana's resentment of her mother, a deeper, darker, bleaker hatred than she had known while growing up as the older of the middle children. "I won't be like you," she whispered at her mother's picture, her arms cradling the newborn Joey. "I'll be proud." She resigned from Jingle Junk and set out to conquer motherhood in ninety days—to spite her mother. Soon she discovered there was an art to diapering an infant. And the instruction manual, *What to Expect the First Year*, didn't help. Caretaking was a 24-hour, seven-day-a-week job; it flowed like froth off a boiling pot.

This morning, she bathes Joey after feeding him mashed bananas and oatmeal. He splashes bubbles over the tub. Dana bends to wipe the puddle. Joey squeals and pats the sudsy foam. More water spills onto the linoleum. Dana lays a towel beside the tub and sits on the toilet, bored as a lifeguard on an empty beach. She imagines what her co-workers are writing this month: *Just reduced! Elegant yet economical, 18-karat gold-plated, all-in-one whistle-blowing bird-calling anti-flea repellant cat collar. Only $19.99*. Dana keeps asking herself, Where did my life jump the tracks?

And she keeps thinking back to a dream she had six years ago about a family softball game where she took a called third strike. Her father was pitching and she couldn't swing the bat. The pitch was in the dirt and her mother, who was umpiring, called it a strike. In the third, fourth, and fifth innings, her brothers and sister jeered at her in the outfield while Norman called her a tobacco-chewing rookie in high heels and a mini-skirt. "You can't even swing the bat," he said. "What makes you think you'll score? Give it up, go get a real job. This is your life!"

This is my life. A baby and bubble bath. A husband who's taken a night auditing job so I can stay home and play house.

The telephone rings. It's Herbert, her friend from the Home Shopping Outlet. "Hey, sweety," he says. He's singing and nobody can sing like him, not even an Elvis impersonator. Since her pregnancy, Herbert's called her once a week to keep her updated on adult life outside of Baby Headquarters. He's brought her flowers and asked her on a date, even paying for a sitter. At first, Dana was afraid Norman would be concerned about her visiting with another man, but Norman told her he thinks it's cute the way some guy who gets paid to shop dotes on his wife. Sometimes, when she hasn't had much sleep or hasn't seen Norman for days, Dana imagines Herbert's in love with her. "Sweety," he once told her, "if you weren't married, we'd be writing soap operas together." Now, in a sing-song voice, he tells her, "It's Mothers' Day next week. What would ya like me to get ya?"

"I don't know."

"Come on, sweety, I'm all shook up."

Dana panics, remembering the article she just read about the woman who drowned her daughter. "Can you hold on? Joey's in the tub. It'll only be a minute."

Dana drapes a squirming, squealing Joey over her shoulder and picks up the phone. "Herb?"

"I ain't nothing but a hound dog. You sound distressed. I'll be right over, all right?"

Ten minutes later, Herbert raps three times on Dana's front door. He lives down the street across from the cable company. He's wearing his work attire: an old pin-striped white shirt with a gravy stain above the breast pocket, a pair of faded Levi's that his butt and legs will never properly fill, and imitation leather cowboy boots. He's five inches shorter than Dana, just the right size for her to pick the dandruff off his scalp, and when he leans forward to kiss her cheek, he has to stand on his toes to get it right. He smells of spearmint mouthwash and Old Spice. His face is smooth. He bends down and swings Joey in the air. The boy giggles and wiggles his feet.

"I was working and thinking of you and guess what I saw, the perfect gift: Java bunny. Open the neck, stick in the beans, turn the ears, and whalla! Ground coffee in ten seconds. But when I went to place an order, they were out of stock. So I came over to see what else your little hound dog can get you, sweety."

"I wish you'd stop buying me gifts. It's making me homesick for Jingle Junk." Dana already has a glass curio cabinet in the dining room filled with knickknacks from Herbert: talking pencil sharpeners, walking mugs, and a sunflower that dances to rock music.

"Okay, okay. Only fools rush in. No more gifts." Herbert places Joey on his stomach on the living room carpet. Joey topples on his face, then pushes up with his arms, and falls to the side. Dana kneels and helps him back onto his belly and encourages him to move his arms and legs in synchronization. The child resists.

Dana sighs. "What do you think of Joey? Norman thinks he's fine, but I just read an article about crawling and learning disabilities." She bursts into tears. "I'm scared."

"Here, let me hold you." Herbert's face fits perfectly between her breasts. He buries his nose between them and smells her perfume. Dana eases away from him and dries her eyes. Herbert says, "I wish I could help you, but I don't know nothing about kids." He rocks back and forth on his heels and whistles a few bars of "Blue Moon" before inspiration strikes. "Want to go to the flea market? It might cheer you up." Dana thinks about it. Really, she should be cleaning house or telephoning the Quicksleeper to see if Norman plans on coming home, but the formidable stack of dirty clothes nauseates her.

"Okay, let's go." Dana bundles Joey into a 49'ers sweatshirt and straps him in the car seat in her Dodge minivan. Herbert sits beside her in the passenger's seat, scratching at a pimple under his nose.

The ride is primarily calm and silent, punctuated only with Herbert humming "Let Me Be Your Teddy Bear," and Joey kicking the back of her seat.

At the flea market, Herbert buys a polo shirt, three pairs of used Levi's, and a half-empty bottle of imitation Chanel No. 5 for his mother. Dana pushes Joey back and forth between the narrow tables and marvels at the brightly colored articles. How would she describe them in a glossy 24-page brochure? Then she glances at Joey who's managed to grab the edge of a tablecloth. She swats his hand and he scrunches up his face and cries. Then Dana cries. "I hate being a mother!"

"You don't mean that." Herbert rubs his hand up and down Dana's back. "You just need a vacation. Let's go to the beach."

"When?"

"Right now."

Dana thinks about it—the article mentioned something about how a variety of textures helps activate different parts of children's brains—and then she agrees, thinking the gritty sand between Joey's toes might motivate him to crawl.

At the beach Herbert sings, "I can't help falling in love with you," and asks, "Will you marry me?"

Dana is flabbergasted. She lets Joey slip out of her hands. He rolls over and over until his body disappears in the waves.

"Joey! Joey! Somebody help!"

A young man with his shirt off and well-molded pectorals dives into the waves and rescues the baby. He carries the limp body to shore and pumps the water out of his lungs and gives him mouth-to-mouth. Dana clasps her hands and trembles, thinking of what Norman might say if he knew, but then Herbert rubs his hand up and down her back, and she tells him, "No, I won't marry you."

Joey opens his eyes and rolls onto his belly and starts to crawl toward two older children building a sand castle. His palms and knees mold tracks in the wet sand. Dana turns to the young man who resuscitated Joey. His body glistens from the fresh salt water. Beads of moisture trickle from his hair; it is the kind of blond that shines in your hands. "Thank you for saving my son's life. You have great hair."

"Thanks." The young man runs his fingers through his slick dark-blond curls. "I owe it to Black Tar Hair Cream with vegetable oil. I would have never bought it, if it hadn't been for this zany television commercial about a monkey with dandruff."

Dana's eyes brighten. "*I* wrote that ad."

"Then we're even," the young man says. "You saved my hair and I saved your son's life."

Dana smiles and imagines sea monkeys floating in the blues of the young man's eyes. Dana falls in love with her future—Black Tar Hair Cream and a crawling Joey—and offers her arm to the young man. Together, they walk off into the sunset toward Joey who is crawling over the children's hands as they shape sand into turrets, and in the distance, they hear Herbert singing, "Don't Be Cruel" to an old man as he jogs by.

Randy Returns

When Howard died, I didn't cry. You think I would have, being his wife for thirteen years, his girlfriend for two more, but I couldn't find a wet spot on my face no matter what anyone said or did. It was as if my whole life had frozen, and nothing could break through the ice and free me to be me again.

I stopped writing the novel I had been working on for the last several months and had to call my agent to ask for an extension. "It's grief," I told her, although it was a lie. I had not grieved one bit.

On the morning of the funeral, I stood between my in-laws, Mr. and Mrs. Wright, two pillars of elegance. Mr. Wright wore an imported Italian suit of the finest light wool. His diamond cuff links glinted in the late September sunlight. Mrs. Wright wore a black Prada dress with her Jimmy Choos. My ten-year-old son, Stephen, stood in front of me wearing a dark blue suit with his father's favorite pin-striped tie with silver and navy silk threads. I felt frumpy in my black sweater and baggy slacks wearing scuffed up Mary Janes, but I never saw a reason to shop since I worked from home.

My best friend, Meg, stood next to us. She looked like Audrey Hepburn in her black slip dress and pillbox hat over her short blond hair, the color of new hay. She dabbed her wet cheeks with a handkerchief she purchased at the vintage store across the street from the church. She always had a crush on Howard, and not surprisingly, his death affected her more than it affected me, although I went to bed with him every night and woke up with him every morning.

When the pastor announced for us to say our farewells, Stephen and I walked up and laid a bouquet of red roses on the closed coffin. "Bye, Dad," Stephen said, touching the wood. "I love you."

I swallowed, unable to speak.

The guests lined up to pay their last respects. A figure emerged from the distance: dark sports jacket over a white T-shirt, faded denim jeans, and black hiking boots. Soon the features of a face became distinct. He had long salt and pepper hair pulled into a low pony tail, crazy cat's eyes the color of topaz and jade, and John Lennon glasses. The man removed a bottle of vodka from a paper bag and placed it at the foot of the coffin. "Drink up, buddy," he whispered.

Mr. Wright strode over to the man. "Mr. Wilson, do not desecrate the memory of my son," he said in a low and steady voice.

Randy, who none of us had seen since he left on a musical scholarship to Bali over ten years ago, smirked. "No disrespect, sir. Just provisions for the afterlife."

Mr. Wright lifted the bottle and tossed it toward the grassy knoll.

Randy loped away, chasing it like a dog asked to fetch.

***

After the funeral, Meg ushered me from the retreating crowd of weeping relatives and consoling friends. We stood on a knoll beside an old oak tree. Stephen had wandered off to read the names of deceased strangers on flat tombstones.

"Who invited Randy?" Meg demanded.

I shrugged. "I don't know. He just showed up."

"How appropriate of him," Meg said, rolling her eyes. "He pretends none of us exists and then when one of us dies, he comes for the cookies and punch afterward."

"You don't know that, Meg."

"And you know why he showed up?"

"He probably heard about it from one of our mutual friends or read the announcement in the obituaries and decided to come because he cares."

"I thought he was dead."

"Most people did."

The rumor was Randy had died, drunk in Bali.

The truth was he was strolling over the grassy knoll toward us.

"How impudent," Meg hissed.

I grabbed her arm. "You're not leaving, are you?"

"I don't intend on talking to him. I have nothing to say."

"He was your boyfriend for Christ's sake."

"That was years ago. I've never forgiven him for the way he treated you while you were pregnant."

"He did nothing unkind."

Meg eased back and bumped into the tree trunk. Randy towered before us, six feet of skin and bone. He was gaunter than I had remembered him, but a smoother, quieter expression creased the lines of his face. His hair was graying and one of his teeth had rotted into black, from too much drinking, I guessed. I thought he had come to talk to Meg, to apologize for his behavior years ago, but it was me he looked at with those crazy eyes: one green, the other gold. "I'm sorry about Howie," he said. He placed his fingers in the belt loops of his faded jeans. A cool autumn breeze blew open the black sports jacket, exposing his tight chest and trim waist. "How're you doing? Holding up?"

I nodded.

"Is that the little guy?" he asked, nodding behind me.

I turned. Stephen knelt before a tombstone and rubbed away the dirt. His brown hair fell in a long fringe around his round face. "Yes, that's Stephen Randolph Wright."

"Right on." Randy flashed a crooked smile. "You named him after me."

"Of course."

Meg cleared her throat. "I'll meet you at your parents' house," she said, touching my elbow. I opened my arms to her for a hug. She embraced me, a hollow circle, and brushed my cheek with her cool lips. "Good-bye."

"Bye, Meggy," Randy said. His gaze slithered down the length of her body, from her sharp collar bones to her slender calves and tiny feet. "You're looking good."

Her blue eyes narrowed. I thought she might snap at him like she was wont to do. But she folded her arms under her breasts, bowed her head, and walked away toward the parking lot.

The breeze carried the scent of roses and newly mown grass. I rubbed my nose to prevent a sneeze. Randy stared at me, not through me. Years melted away. I should have felt like a thirty-five-year old widow facing middle age alone. Instead, I felt fifteen, ready to sneak out of my parents' house and party until the break of dawn.

Randy gazed at something behind me, maybe Stephen, maybe nothing. "I don't think Meggy's very happy to see me. Most people probably aren't, but I'm in town for a few days, and I have nowhere to go. I thought maybe I could stay with you, if you don't mind, or I could borrow some money for a motel."

I nodded. "Sure. You could stay with us. Let me get Stephen." I called out to my son. Stephen stood up and ran over to us. I moved to brush his bangs out of his brown eyes, but he swiped my hand aside.

"Are we going to Grandma's?" He squinted at Randy. "Aren't you the guy who made Grandpa mad?"

Randy held out his hand to Stephen. "I'm Randolph Woodrow Wilson, Jr. But you can call me Randy. I was your father's best friend from high school."

Stephen cocked his head and squinted as if the sun had burst through the dense clouds. He had heard stories of Randy, mostly from Meg.

Whenever a report about juvenile delinquency or drug and alcohol abuse, unemployment, and homelessness surfaced in the news, Meg would say, "Just like Randy," as though it held the validity of a national statistic. The name became an obscenity, and Stephen recognized it for what it was.

"Randy's coming home with us," I said, trying hard to make it sound better than it was.

"Why? Is he homeless?"

"Stephen, apologize."

"For what? Speaking the truth?"

"Randy cares about us."

"Yeah, then why wasn't he there when I was born or growing up like Meg was? Why'd he show up now?"

"Stephen, watch your mouth."

Randy placed his hand on my wrist. "I don't have to come. I can stay at a motel."

"Nonsense. I haven't seen you in years. There's so much catching up to do."

"He's not staying in my room," Stephen said.

"Listen, Jude. I'll get a motel."

"But you don't have—"

"Listen, don't worry. The kid's on to me."

"You bet I am," Stephen said. "You're a loser."

I slapped Stephen's cheek. His mouth twisted like he was going to cry, but he either caught himself or thought better of it. He spat at Randy's feet before darting up the knoll to the parking lot where Meg opened the door of her Ford Focus. Stephen grabbed Meg's elbow and spun around pointing at us.

"I'm sorry," I apologized again to Randy.

"No, kid's right. I was those things. Still am. Sometimes." He winked.

Suddenly my heart ached. It ached from losing Howard. It ached from seeing Randy again.

I had been calm during the last week, from the moment of Howard's seizure to the moment of the pastor's final words. But when Randy appeared, something dislodged inside of me. For the first time, I cried. The tears jerked out of me, stubborn and unrehearsed.

Without a word, Randy folded me against his chest. I could feel the warmth of his skin through his thin T-shirt. It made me feel safe and at home. His gentle fingertips stroked my hair as he rocked me slightly from side to side. I thought he was whispering hush, but he was humming a song, a song he and Howard had written when they were part of the band, *White Demons,* during college. It was the song Randy had hummed in Chili's Bar and Grill the night I last saw him over ten years ago; the night Meg broke up with him. The night Randy moved far away and no one heard from him again. The freshness of the memory jolted me and I pulled away, wiping my eyes with the back of my hand.

I glanced up at the parking lot to make sure no one was watching before I opened my purse and removed all the cash in my wallet. I shoved it into Randy's palm and said, "The Extended Stay is within walking distance. Don't go to the Hilton. That's where Howard's relatives are staying tonight."

Randy shoved the money into his front pocket. "I'll call you sometime next week to see how you're doing, if that's okay with you?"

"Yes, it is. We're in the phone book." As I watched Randy leave, I felt a bolt of warmth spread down from my scalp to the small of my back as I remembered the tenderness of his fingertips as they curled around the crumpled bills I had offered him.

***

Randy, as promised, did call one week later. His voice, low and concerned, crackled over the bad connection and I had to call him back. When our lines connected, he inquired about our health and wondered if there was anything we needed.

"No, we're fine," I lied. Stephen was doing poorly in school, picking fights on the playground, refusing to complete assignments, staring sullenly at the blackboard when his turn was called to answer a question on fractions and decimals. His teacher, Mrs. Yokomata, suggested grief counseling. Meg agreed.

"I know a colleague who specializes in families in mourning. I refer a lot of clients to her. You should make an appointment for next week," Meg said over the phone when I told her about Stephen.

"I don't know if we can afford it."

"Tell her I referred you and she'll give you a discount." Meg's voice lowered a notch. "If it'll help, I'll pay for the first couple of sessions as a gift in memory of Howard."

"That's sweet of you, Meg, but—"

"Go." She was insistent. "Howard would want you to." And, she was right. He would.

I scheduled an appointment for Tuesday afternoon.

When Randy called, I sat in a white terry cloth robe at the breakfast bar in the stainless steel kitchen drinking black coffee with a mountain of paperwork: life insurance, living trust, stock certificates, death certificate. I welcomed the distraction.

Stephen had walked to the school bus alone, something he preferred to do at this age, first having outgrown the need for an adult, and now feeling he was the man of the family. He had grown strangely protective of me since the funeral, almost to the point of ridiculousness. He would tell me what Dad would have wanted me to do, refusing to obey me when I called him to dinner, asked him to do his homework or get ready for bed. He said how ashamed he was to have a stranger appear at Dad's funeral, not the friend I had known Randy to be, not as the friend I still considered him.

"Where are you staying?" I asked Randy, coveting this rare moment of us alone.

"Behind Dick's Diner next to the dumpster, but I'm calling from the gas station. It's the only pay phone I could find."

I should have known the money wouldn't last a week. I thought about the extra room downstairs across from the laundry room. It had been Howard's office. I could clear it out and offer it to Randy.

"Listen, I know your kid doesn't like me. Hell, not many people do, but I was wondering if I could come by, clean up, and shave."

"Sure. I'll pick you up."

I slipped on an old pair of jeans, a bit too snug around my thickening waist, and tugged one of Howard's T-shirts over my head. I pulled my hair into a pony tail and fastened it with a rubber band, knowing it would hurt when I yanked it out later that night but not caring. I wanted to see Randy again.

The Honda's old engine roared and hummed. I drove downtown past the brick and mortar high school with its wrought iron entrance and circular driveway and oak trees; past the drug store with its face lift of red and white paint, and pulled into the gas station. Randy smiled, a wild squiggly line, and uncurled from where he squatted against the wall. His black and gray hair matted against his scalp, a three day growth sprouted against the flat planes of his cheeks, and his T-shirt clung to his chest with sweat, dirt and kitchen grease. He slung a knapsack over one shoulder, a dark sports jacket over the other. I leaned over and opened the passenger's door. Randy tucked himself into the seat and slammed the door.

"Thanks, Jude. You're a lifesaver." He leaned over and pecked my cheek. He smelled of spoiled milk and day old bread and vodka. "I would've called sooner, but I didn't have the change."

"So, where to after this?" I asked.

"Hell, I don't know. I thought I'd cruise into town and look you guys up, stay a few days and be on my way north. Oregon. Washington. Canada. Alaska. Finish my tour across America, you know. I'd thought I'd surprise Howie so I called his office and the receptionist says he doesn't work there anymore. He passed away yesterday. I thought she was yanking my leg, so I Googled his name at the library and, hell, it's right there under an ad for hair replacement cream. Howard Anthony Wright, 35, died of a brain tumor. Shit, I didn't know what to do. Then I thought I'd show up for the funeral. He was my friend, you know, don't care what anyone says."

"I'm sorry about the poor reception, but you have to admit, your entrance was unexpected."

Randy laughed and slapped his thighs. "Hell, I'll never forget old man Wright's face when I laid the bottle down. I thought he was going to blow a blood vessel."

I smirked, amused in spite of myself. Who else would offer alcohol instead of flowers? Only dear ol' Randy. "How long are you going to stay?" I asked.

"Hell, I'll be out before your kid's home, if that's what you mean."

"No," I laughed, and patted Randy's knee. "I didn't mean that. Stephen's just a little upset. He loved his father."

"Yeah, yeah, yeah. The kid's angry. Hell, the whole town is, or so it seems." He lifted his glasses and rubbed the sleep out of his eyes. "No, I won't be here too long. Nothing left, now." Then, as if the thought just occurred to him, he turned to me and asked, "Why?"

"Well," I cleared my throat and gripped the steering wheel tighter. I didn't know how to say what I wanted to say, but I wasn't about to let the opportunity pass and spend another ten years wondering what could have been. "There's an extra room downstairs, Howard's office, which you could have if you were going to stay." I held my breath.

Randy licked his upper lip and rested his arm against the ledge of the window. "You know that's not a good idea, don't you?"

I shrugged. It didn't seem like a bad idea. "I don't like the idea of you sleeping on the streets."

"Yeah, I am getting a little old for it." He stretched his arms with fingers linked and cracked his knuckles.

At the house, I pulled the car into the driveway beside the sprawling green lawn. I led Randy through the back yard. Randy lifted his long legs in exaggerated steps to avoid trampling on Howard's vegetable garden, even though most of the tomato plants had withered in the week since his death. I was not much of a gardener and even the simplest of things like watering escaped me. Inside, I showed Randy to the bathroom upstairs in the bedroom I had shared with Howard. Not being much of a housekeeper, the bed was unmade and the dresser was cluttered with notes from midnight inspiration. I grabbed clean towels and tossed him Howard's plush red robe to wear while I washed his clothes. Nothing else of Howard's would fit him, I was sure. Howard topped out at five-feet, eight-inches compared to Randy's six-feet. Howard weighed at least thirty pounds more, give or take a few pounds.

I listened to the door close and Randy's sweet voice, humming while he undressed and tossed the soiled T-shirt and underwear into a pile outside the door. I gathered the clothes and the knapsack and paraded downstairs into the laundry room, sorting the colors from the whites just as Howard had shown me the first year we were married. "No bleach," Howard said, laying his hand over my wrist. "These are silk. I'll hand wash them. And these need to go into a net bag," he said, referring to my nylons. I had resented him then, but now I was grateful. His unsolicited advice helped me avoid shrunken clothes, faded colors, and shredded stockings.

At the bottom of Randy's knapsack, amid the loose dirt and pennies, were matchbooks and trial-sized bars of soap with the names of hotels and restaurants. They marked his trail across the country. I caressed each one, turning them over in the palm of my hand, reading every word, breathing in the scent of deodorant soap through the stiff plastic-coated paper wrappers and examining the perfect white heads of the matches. Things he had never used. I closed my eyes and imagined the thrill and excitement Randy must have experienced moving from city to city, taking whatever he needed before moving on. And all those years, everyone thought he was dead, including me.

"Hullo, hullo, hullo." Randy draped his arm up the side of the doorjamb and leaned into the frame.

"Where haven't you been?" I asked.

"England. To see the queen." He bowed before me. When he stood up, his black and gray hair fell in thin wet tendrils around his shoulders. I thought of Medusa with her head full of snakes. Randy grasped my fingers and brought my hand to his lips. "Me lady."

I chuckled. "My lord."

I started the first load of whites, underwear, T-shirts, and socks.

Randy followed me, a slender shadow, down the hall, past the dining room, and into the kitchen. "Hungry?" I asked.

"Famished, me lady."

I opened up the refrigerator, poured a glass of orange juice, and handed it to him while I fixed some toast. He eyed the glass, the pulp floating to the bottom, and said, "Too bad I finished my last pint. Could've had a screwdriver for breakfast."

"Do you usually drink?"

"When I went to rehab, I discovered alcohol is my Higher Power." Randy snatched the toast out of my hand and sauntered out of the kitchen. He peered into each room, examining the china cabinet in the dining room with the polished silver and Waterford crystal which was seldom used, then exiting into the living room with its plush white carpet and matching sofa and love seat in soft linen the color of sand in Hawaii. His fingers caressed the oak cabinet housing our entertainment center, stereo, and big screen TV.

Then he found the iPod. He slapped his hands together instead of wiping the crumbs on the robe. He shuffled through the songs. A familiar guitar chord preceded the Beatles singing, "Can't Buy Me Love."

The phone rang. I darted into the hall and picked it up on the third ring. It was Meg. Randy whooped and hollered, "She loves you, yeah, yeah, yeah." He sprung from the cushions of the couch and danced barefoot on the glass coffee table. I turned down the volume. Randy sang louder. "Hello?" I cupped my hand over the mouth of the handset and darted into the kitchen.

"What's all the ruckus?" Meg asked.

"Randy's over."

"You let him into your house?"

"He was dirty and hungry."

"That's no reason."

"Meg, he's not a stray cat. He's a human being." Randy bounced into the room. His arms slipped around my waist. He nuzzled his face against my cheek. I giggled.

"What's so funny?" Meg demanded.

"Meggy?" His hot breath warmed against the skin near my eyes. I blinked. "May I?" He reached for the phone.

I wriggled out of his arms and darted back into the living room. "Why'd you call?" I wanted to keep the conversation brief.

"I wanted to see if you were all right. Did you make an appointment with Catherine?"

"Stephen and I see her at 3:30 on Tuesday."

"How long is Randy staying? Not overnight, I hope."

"As long as he wants." I hung up without saying goodbye.

Randy corned me near the sofa. "How come you didn't let me talk to her?"

I breathed in deeply, hoping to stop the thoughts from flying out of my mouth. But I had spent the majority of my life keeping my feelings for Randy a secret and I wasn't about to anymore. "She doesn't love you, dammit, and I do." I pushed past him. My whole body trembled as I unloaded the whites, tossed them into the dryer, and started the final load. The water plunked through the pipes and rushed into the tub. The comforting swish-swish of the agitator calmed my nerves.

Randy stood in the doorway. "Jude?"

My voice cracked into a sob. "I love you more than I could ever love Howard."

"You don't know what you're saying."

"I know exactly what I'm saying." I held his gaze, as if I had the power to never let him go. "Why didn't you keep in touch?"

Randy sighed. "I need a drink."

"No, you don't. You need to tell me the truth."

He lifted his sleeve. A railroad of scars traveled up his arm. I traced the tracks with my finger. The skin was raised and hard like a callous.

"Don't ask me to talk about it," he said. "It's not my happy time."

"What happened to your music?"

"No stamina." He shrugged. "Sure, I can jam on stage for a few sets, but to do it every night, night after night, becomes a job. And I was never good at keeping a job. Now I live to drink, and drink to live."

I wrapped my arms around him and buried my face against the terry cloth covering his chest. If I had been with Randy all these years, who would I have become? An indolent writer fueled by alcohol, or a homeless poet seeking shelter from the stinging rain?

Randy lifted my chin until I met his gaze. "I remember why I like you."

"And why is that?" I expected nothing deep.

Randy tipped his head to the side and smiled. "You see things outside the box. Even though you live in the box."

My heart sank. "I never wanted to live in the box."

"I know." Randy lifted me up and set me on the dryer. When we kissed, I closed my eyes and breathed in his breath and imagined what my life would have looked like if I had chosen to live as someone else.

***

Hours later, I woke to Stephen's anxious hands shaking my shoulders. "Mom, what happened?"

I sat up on the living room carpet. My back was stiff and my muscles were sore. The last thing I remembered was falling asleep in Randy's arms. I rubbed my neck, wondering where Randy was.

"Did someone break in and rob us?" Stephen asked.

The coffee table had been pushed aside. The pillows from the sofa were scattered on the floor. The iPod was missing from the charging dock.

"Did someone hurt you?"

I glanced down at my rumpled clothes, the shirt pulled half-way over my shoulders and the unbuttoned crotch of my pants. What explanation could I offer my son?

The front door swung open and heels clip-clopped against the tiles and dissolved into the plush carpet. Meg's arms wrapped around my back and her sobs shuddered against me, "Oh, God, no, no, no."

I pushed her away, shaking my head. "I'm all right," I reassured her. "I just fell asleep. No one hurt me. I'm okay."

"But you look like you've been attacked."

Although I was a bit disorientated, pieces of the events leading up to this moment floated back to me like flotsam and jetsam after a storm. Randy, carrying me out of the laundry room. My legs wrapped around his waist. Falling onto the sofa. Smothering each other in kisses.

"Why do you have that silly look on your face?" Meg demanded. Then a glint of recognition flickered in her blue eyes. "It was Randy, wasn't it? He did this." Meg stalked into the dining room and gasped about missing silverware and crystal candle holders. "What else did he steal?" She rummaged through the house, room to room, and detailed the missing items to me like a police report: Howard's gold and diamond cuff-links, my pearl earrings and necklace, a silver-plated letter opener, a mother-of-pearl comb, Stephen's collectible baseball cards and stamp collection. Anything small and vaguely valuable was gone.

"I want my baseball cards back," Stephen said.

"I don't think you'll ever get them back," Meg said, stroking his head. "Unless you frequent pawn shops in the wrong section of town."

But I wasn't concerned about the missing things. I was concerned about Randy. I straightened my clothes and stood up, ready to call for a search and rescue party. "Where is he?"

"Gone," Meg said.

I checked the laundry room. The washer was empty. The door to the dryer was open. Not an item of clothing was found. Suddenly I felt cold. I hugged my arms to stop from shaking. If I left now, could I find him?

Meg sent Stephen into the kitchen for an afternoon snack. When she returned, I had slipped on a pair of sneakers and grabbed a sweater from the closet in Howard's office.

"Where are you going?" she asked.

"To find him."

Meg grabbed my hand and screamed. "That bastard stole your wedding ring!"

I glanced at my fingers. Meg was right. The third finger of my left hand was bare. Gone was the one-carat princess-cut diamond ring Howard had saved six months to buy me.

"I think we should call the police and file charges," Meg said.

I stared at the pale skin where my ring had been. I was no longer married to Howard, just as I was no longer married to the What Ifs of the past. All my questions had been answered. All my doubts had been erased.

While Meg called the police on her cell phone, I wandered into the kitchen and sat down next to Stephen who was dipping apple slices in a jar of peanut butter. He had his father's eyes and my sad smile. I ruffled his hair and said, "We'll get your baseball cards back."

He glanced up at me and stopped chewing. "Really?"

Even if we had to scour every pawn shop from here to Alaska, I would find those baseball cards. And my wedding ring.

"Really," I said.

Acknowledgments

"Ashes to Angels," *Potpourri*, 2000

"Fistful of Love," *Visibilities*, 2000

"A Toast Good-bye," *Creativity Connection*, 1999

"Angels in Underwear," *Bookrix.com*, 2009

"Lips," *Foliate Oak*, 2001

"Special," *Women's Voices*, 2000

"Cut Above the Rest," *Abundance Press*, 1999

"Heatwave," *Literary Potpourri*, 2000, reprinted in *Rose and Thorn*, 2001

"Friends," *Blithe House Quarterly*, 2001

"Out of Focus," *Foliate Oak*, 2002

"Queen of Jingle Junk," *Lynx Eye*, 1996

About the Author

During her more than 20-year career, Angela Lam has entertained and educated readers through poems, articles, essays, and novels. *The Human Act and Other Stories* showcases fourteen of her best, award-winning short stories, including "Lips," which was nominated for a Pushcart Prize, "Ashes to Angels," a semi-finalist for fiction from the Heekin Group Foundation, and "A Toast Good-Bye," which won first place in *Creativity Connection*'s fiction contest.

A native of California, she is also the author of two chick lit novels (*Legs* and *Out of Balance*) and a paranormal thriller (*Blood Moon Rising*) all published as Angela Lam Turpin.

Visit her at www.angelalamturpin.com.

ALL THINGS THAT MATTER PRESS ™

FOR MORE INFORMATION ON TITLES AVAILABLE FROM
ALL THINGS THAT MATTER PRESS, GO TO
http://allthingsthatmatterpress.com
or contact us at
allthingsthatmatterpress@gmail.com